I0722021

JĀNA

a novel

by

Mi'Kha-el Feeza

1st Edition

Book 1 of 3

Woman OF

Santa Monica

California

a "RA Specialty, Inc." project

羽 很不朽 **Publishing Company**

**Book Age Appropriate Rating:
PG-23 (Parental Guidance till Age 23)**

Please respect the Integrity of the artist so that the artist can continue to thrive to bring you more works of art!

Piracy affects both the livelihood of the author, publisher, and all those that have collaborated to bring you this piece of art. Thank you!

EF Publishing Book 1 of 3 of Jana Trilogy Novel International Identification Alpha/Number:

7March1968JanaTriologyBook1of3RT13APRIL1950-PB

Everlasting Feather Publishing Company (EF Publishing) WEBSITE:

EverlastingFeather.Com

Thank you for your support! Jana Trilogy **eBook available**. Check with your favorite Book App or contact us.

‖‖

Mi'Kha-el Feeza WEBSITE:

Eternoi.Com

Buenos días Reader!

Regeneration of Love and Resistance for the common good is working at my website. We are looking for like-minded individuals and organizations to collectively help tackle the ills of our communities in this world to bring true change peacefully to all its inhabitants! If you'd like to join one of our committees, please do so! We are a true Volunteer Based organization. Every Member is a Volunteer, including leadership! Sincerely, Mi'Kha-el Feeza

eternoi@protonmail.com

This book is dedicated to

the *Charismatic* **Tejano**:

Martin Núñez Soto

A man who loved his family and who loved to
watch and play baseball:
the **Texan** way:)!

We will be together one day my brother

J ā n a

Table of Contents

PART 1 of 7
JANA TRAVELS THROUGH TIME

PART **3** of 7
A MIXTURE OF PLEASURE AND PAIN

PART **1** of 7
JANA TRAVELS THROUGH TIME

Chapter One
An Introduction To Jana

It had been the third time in a week Jana had locked herself out! Jana didn't understand what was going on *IN HER HEAD*!

Luckily, Jana had kept a spare key in the outside *body*-of-the-car, held by a *magnetic box*.

For the last *7* weeks Jana was also not able to understand her sleepless nights...sleeping only between *3* and *4* hours a day!

Weeks Weeks Weeks of insomnia!

Jana knew she needed to do something about all this *t i r e d -n ess* in her head.

Jana decided to change her way of thinking...

She wanted to *think differently* for a better her!

...a more peaceful her.

"A BETTER ME!" Jana SHOUTed in her mind!

As part of this desired *change* Jana needed and desired to add physical exercise...wanting to go to the gym more often: at least to run for 30 minutes on the treadmill.

Jana had-been without-motivation for quite some time...at least at the unconscious level of processing information.

In fact, Jana went back to her daily donut-eating-night-snacks which was not doing well for her weight.

At 5 feet 6 inches, Jana's ideal weight was 134 pounds.

Jana had gained, in less than three weeks, about 20 pounds past her ideal.

Jana could not understand it. Rather, she didn't want to understand it! (..at *that* moment in her life.)

Jana was trying to run away from her *mind!* (from her past!)

Being a present-woman-from-*Los-Angeles*-California, Jana felt she needed to continuously maintain multi-tasking in order to achieve all the goals she had set out for herself.

Busy Busy Busy was the name of the game for all those in Los Angeles...little time for anything else.

Seeking time to relax and reflect was a luxury for most! (*that* included Jana)

Jana's achievement level was down: she was achieving less every day!

Was Jana in rebellion from the norm?

Or was Jana breaking down like an `old-unKept-car?!!!`

Jana was not old...or at least she thought she wasn't. Humanly aged at 34 she sometimes felt

ancient. Literally! Her body sometimes felt like it had been on this Earth for over 2,000 years!

Not meeting the fast-paced-non-stop-quota-of-

Los-Angeles was leading Jana into a **deep** depression.

Jana still-believed-in-the-**system** set-up for her and for all: to obey and to follow....

...that was Jana's *prescribed* standard! That was everyone's standard!

...Any Disobedients were finely-*punished* by the **system** in many direct and indirect ways...including a loss of income for survival in the **system**!...

...Those at the top were the exception to a certain extent. Those at the "top" did not include teachers, lawyers, architects, managers, production crews, doctors, nurses, and so forth.

Who really defined this **system**?

A **system** one is born-into!

Changing the **system** in a standard-straightforward manner was virtually impossible for most [including the author of this book].

The controllers of the **system** did not share the power for fear of loss of power. Or, was this madness to CONTROL for another reason?

Irrespective of the reason, it was their way and their plan and nothing else...even if their plan was not beneficial to the masses or to themselves!

A **CRAZY** set-up!

Democracy! ...a fallacy propagated by those in power at the very top to help the situation from going to complete Chaos!

...And to justify:

...forced CONFORMITY!

A forced deceit!

Jana felt **ALONE** and **ISOLATED**.

At 34 years old, Jana had not been with a man for-over-three-FREAKING-years!

Since her divorce four years ago, Jana had slept only once with a man she met at a night club.

In her mind on-that-night in the nightclub Jana needed to go for the "REBOUND".

Unfortunately, after that brief night-of-bliss in her SUV: Jana felt empty again.

No-real-relationship.

Jana wanted a CONTINUAL passion-burst from the combining-of-energies.

That brief one-night-stand experience only left her wanting more and needing more!

Jana could not find the right-man.

Jana's so-called-friends had set her up on several blind dates: yet she did not find her match.

Now, in this stressful period of her life, Jana was...

alone.

alone.

alone!

No one to hold on to:

...to hold her, to comfort her.

The so-called-*friends* only came over if Jana was willing to go out clubbing with them. Otherwise, they never called or showed.

Jana soon realized that she had *no-true*-friends.

Jana was **ALL-ALONE**-in-**this**-*City-of-Angels*.

Her childhood family was all back in Oklahoma.

Jana did not keep in touch with them on a continual basis as she had hoped in doing so.

Jana needed and wanted more social contact.

Somehow through a web-of-**labyrinths** Jana was not finding her way to-this-goal.

Somehow?

Jana often analyzed her life\herself!

"Where did I go wrong in my past decisions?"

No children were perceivable in the future.

Jana wanted to bear children but with whom?

Jana was regularly unable to clearly understand her decisions and actions when it came to her happiness.

Happiness

Jana was often caught up in her professional career as a classroom high school teacher. She was getting tired of teaching Spanish and wanted a change in this aspect of her life.

Jana wanted to do something different but didn't know how!

In fact, Jana didn't know what it was she wanted to do different.

Scrambled Eggs In The Head!

[Literally!]

Jana's only present vision was to continue to do what she had been doing for the past 11 years.

Jana had a variety of professional-interests she considered in pursuing: unfortunately none could sustain her financially...so Jana discounted them from her options completely.

Jana was in a trench of *no-clear*-opportunities for a better *existence*!

Chapter Two
The Apartment

Well, it was getting late when Jana found her
hidden keys. Fortunately, Jana was able to
remember where she had placed them on the car.

It was about 8 p.m., Mars-day, *September 11*,
2007. Her work week had just started and Jana
had decided to go to **café KKanaKoluKKūMāhā**
for some coffee, and to read the local paper. Jana
liked to read the entertainment section since she
had always liked the arts of creativity---*everything*
from visual to auditory art.

Jana arrived at her apartment sleepy and ready to
hit the sack. She lived in a modest one-bedroom
apartment on the *second* floor of a *9* unit building;
the apartment was just off Ocean Park Blvd on
Euclid in the City of Santa Monica.

Jana loved to *live* as close to the ocean as possible.
It was beautiful to her---the temperatures were
often cool or warm on summer days.

During the winter it did not get too cold like in
Okla*homa*.

Her long walks on the beach boardwalk brought Jana peace in a hectic environment like that found in the County of *Los Angeles*.

Such aerobic activity by the ocean really relieved Jana from most of her stressful thoughts.

As Jana walked into her apartment, she noticed her cat *racing* towards her.

The lights of her apartment were set on a *timer*.

The only light on was the living room corner lamp that was set at *dim*.

Jana bent down to greet the cat with arms wide open.

Jana was able to immediately hug her feline, since she had left all her school stuff (lesson-plans-to-update, files, etc.) in the car.

Jana was too tired to do any work that night.

"I have no one to talk to", she thought, "except me and my *cat*!".

Jana hugged her cat and herself!

Jana walked to the television set and turned it on.

She *drown*ed herself in the *sounds coming* from it.

Jana undressed and headed straight to the bathroom where she turned on the shower.

After a brief rinse, Jana toweled herself and stepped out onto the master bedroom (which was really just slightly bigger than a small room).

Jana was going to check the fridge and suddenly stopped...staring at her naked body in front of the hallway mirror which was held by two wooden legs.

Jana looked at herself.

Jana was of Irish and Native American decent. She knew nothing of her Irish background except that they were at one point connected to a family hundreds of years old that was now in hiding!

All *connection* to her Irish ancestry was lost in the traditional sense.

Her mother Doris was Irish and her father Wild Feather was Comanche.

Like most Native American descendants, Jana's father's culture had been *destroy*ed by the American Imperialist's expansion to the West (which began in Europe and through the oceans of the world and to the lands of the Americas!).

A practice of Manifest Destiny!

Jana's father knew little about the Comanche's true way of life...for that had vanished by the time Wild Feather came-into-this-world!

Undressed, Jana continued looking at herself.

Jana had a couple of flabs...yet she was not exceedingly overweight.

Jana had gone to the gym in the past. Lately however, she lost interest in her *outer* appearance.

Jana stood there looking at herself.

Looking, looking, looking.

What was she?

What was her life about?

What was she supposed to do with her life?

"I mean truly", she spoke aloud.

Jana had the bad-habit of contemplating such questions: of judging herself too much.

Jana judged herself in everything including how she spoke to people, as to what she was thinking, how she should act, what was the proper etiquette, her walk, and so on and so on.

An apparent slave to a perceived etiquette.

Jana had this *bad habit* since childhood...fed by the stupid customs or mental controls of societies!

Jana felt caged in a WHIRL-OF-SELF-EXAMINATION...

... Judging herself to the point where she could not make any real relationships because of her continual *withdrawal* from people who befriended her.

Jana was at a lost...

...not knowing *how* to be happy.

...not knowing *when* to be happy!

Jana had seen a psychologist in the past: it did not help.

Jana also tried reading about how to become happy using self-help books: none of them worked for her. (It appears that the *premise* behind them were not valid...even though from face-value they made sense!).

Nothing worked not now, not yesterday, not never----up to this point in Jana's life.

She was in *stalemate*!

Jana continued to *s*tare at herself as she woke from her thoughts: Jana was *t*an, light br*o*wn skin with an average b-cu*p*ped-breast-size.

In the past Jana had thought of having implants to make herself more attractive. At the end, she voted against it.

"I will be who I am", Jana told herself.

Jana was not an ugly woman.

She had long, light brown hair to her waist. Her body was firm, despite her complaints of a little flab around her abdomen.

Jana had a full blossom-of-brownish-red pubic hair around her vagina. It was very bushy. Jana had thought of shaving it, but she felt she needed to keep her groin area covered.

Jana was not shy and she frequently walked around her apartment naked.

Jana loved to feel the freedom of *being* nude.

She valued freedom (and freedom without restrictions): although Jana was often *a-slave-to-*her-negative-thoughts...which presented a contradiction that barred her from true freedom of mind and body and spirit.

Despite an outgoing personality, Jana was always alone: it was rare that she had visitors. Jana would suppress her personality into a hermit mindset!

Issues from her past had a hold on her wantings and needs...Jana found it difficult to break free toward her true self...something had pulled her away from her true state her true nature.

Contradictions!

Unconsciously Jana was looking for something...and other humans appeared to pose a distraction in her search of that something!

Jana's only regular liiive companions were her cat Fifona, and the exotic salt-water-fishes in a *16 x 25 x 34* inch boxed-size-aquarium.

Ten fishes in all occupied her *salty-waters*.

Jana had an automatic-feeder that released the fishes' food-flakes on-to-the-living-waters!

If not for this mechanism, there could have been times where the little critters would have been in danger of dying.

Too many things occupied Jana's mind at times where she would overlook important duties like feeding her non-nagging pets, which excluded the cat which was always demanding attention and affection:)!

Jana's face was beautiful: she bore beautiful *grey*ish-brown eyes that were cupped in thinly slanted figures.

Large eyelashes brushed her prominent cheek bones. Her lips were lushes of plumped-red-plums.

Jana wore *dark* lipstick over her gentle-red-lips that needed *no* additional color.

There stood Jana:

........drifting from one thought to the next: letting all her anxieties run through and slowly releasing them as she focused her mind-and-body into images of welcoming-horizons and running-waters!

Jana was seeking a calmer-state-of-mind.

Jana wanted to forget about all her worries and frustrations.

Jana sought a release from a world of fast-

moving-cars, slow-moving-cars, hurried-people, careless-people, and the OPPORTUNISTS wanting to provide unhealthy doses of high-vicious-advertisements... promising a better outcome with the use of their products...

...corporations seeking to gain a profit as to one's insecurities and doubts... opening an opportunity for a "profiteer-*created*" development of wants-and-needs!

Jana *hate*d the pharmaceutical companies the most!

..........Jana did not *believe* that taking a drug for every single discomfort or the apparent lacking of some hormone made people better-in-the-long-run.

If anything, the people who decided to be regular drug users were made dependent on the system prescribed to them.

Jana frowned in disappointment as to these opportunists!

 "We now live in a world of *the pill*", she thought.

"A pill for this and a pill for that---all for the sake of turning a healthy profit...forcing the vulnerable population toward a dependency on something that will not fix 'the problems' associated with any imaginable or created *issue* out there."

"...Pills creating a distraction from the **true-root** of issues adding-more-distractions to an already *distracted world*."

There stood Jana...in a trance-of-thoughts.

S l o w ly Jana fell asleep.

After about five minutes, Jana lost *physical*

control of her *body*...causing-it-to-*tilt*-straight-toward-the-mirror.

Jana came crashing down on it: *breaking* the glass.

Her forgetfulness of where she was had overtaken her...again!

Jana woke from her *concussion* received by hitting the floor.

After a while Jana became aware of her proprioception.

...she became aware and felt herself face down on the broken mirror board.

At that moment of consciousness, Jana didn't quite know *where* she was or *what* had happened.

As Jana opened her eyes, the first thing that she saw was the broken image of herself on the mirror.

After trying to make sense of the situation, Jana realized what had happened.

She carefully proceeded to lift her arms to push herself up.

Luckily for her, Jana had not ripped her skin.

The glass had broken in several places---some more prominent than others. Yet, they kept their position as to the back board that was *behind* the *glass*.

Jana crouched herself up and squatted for a while: feeling a bit of pain on her forehead from the collision.

The cat stood by the door: frightened of hearing ALL-THE-RUCKUS!

Jana s l o w l y stood up.

She was thankful that it wasn't worst.

Over the years, Jana had learned not to freak out about such incidents. She was well trained now. In her mind, Jana thought, "I'll pick it up later".

Jana headed to the bathroom.

As she entered the bedroom toward the bathroom door, Jana immediately noticed that the rug was extremely damp.

"Shit!"...she thought: remembering that she had turned on the tub-faucet...wanting to soak in it for a while after her brief shower.

The bedroom and bathroom floors were flooded with water!

Jana raced to turn off the water.

She acted quickly to fix the *situation*. It was too late...the water had seeped through the floor.

She did not hear a knock-at-the-*door*!

Her downstairs neighbors were apparently not in. Jana grabbed blankets and towels, and whatever else was at her disposal to soak up the water.

Jana laboriously carried these soaked fabrics to the balcony: not being aware that she was still naked!

When-the-situation-normalized SOMEWHAT, Jana went to the dining room table to write a note for the neighbors downstairs... assuring them that she would pay for the *soaky* cleanup and any valuables that may have been *damaged*.

As Jana headed toward the door, she *realize*d that she was nude.

She quickly put some shorts on and a t-shirt and headed downstairs.

Jana *tagged* the door with the note and headed up *stairs*.

Chapter Three
The Gym

Everything seemed to be going well again for Jana!

Then, in Jana's mind, it was becoming sour again: Jana felt mental tension building due to the *water-occurrence* that evening.

Jana attempted to resist her negativity.

She decided to put on some running shoes and head to the local gym.

Jana had not gone to the gym in three years!

Three years!

THREE YEARS!

Her membership had not expired...quietly accumulating debt.

Things aside:

Jana was thinking of an exercise regimen for the night. "Maybe", she thought, "I need to run a while on the treadmill and then head to the Jacuzzi for relaxation".

Fully dressed and on-the-road again Jana drove toward the gym....*twelve* blocks away.

When Jana arrived she was determined not to let her recent misfortune dampen her overall mood.

["dampen" get it!:)...nerd humor!]

Exercising would create AN ESCAPE for Jana.

Jana went into the locker room and sat down.

Jana sat there trying to create the discipline to push forward with her exercise and think of nothing else.

It was a *struggle*.

Jana breathed in...*slowly* and forcefully bringing herself to void-the-world!

V O I D I N G ~~the world~~ !

A mental-blocking of the distractions Jana tried to accomplish while sitting there in a struggle.

Jana put her bag into one of the lockers and headed to the treadmill.

Jana stretched and warmed-up before her run...notifying the body:

It's time!

Jana received a *q*uantacized-***m***il*t*riplets images of-a-single-thought of the many-times she had done this before: how this activity RENEWED her to *feel good.*

Tonight more than ever Jana needed this excellent cardio-vascular activity!

Jana needed a release of **b** a d-energy.

Jana stood on the treadmill.

And then, after several seconds of mental preparation, Jana started slowly...walking at first and eventually *running* at 5 miles an hour.

No incline position---Jana knew that would tire her out and she wanted to run for at least 34 minutes.

Jana wanted a *renewal-of*-her-*strength* and of her **peace**... even though she knew that it was only for a brief moment and that it wouldn't last:

nothing seemed to last: everything needed renewal.

Jana had to get out of her lazy *mode*.

Jana started to run faster.... increasing her pace to 6.1 miles an hour!

Jana began feeling good and breathing well.

Around Jana there were other participants of this cardio-vascular ritual---each in the gym for *different* reasons:

Some wanted to decrease body mass to fit the image-of-fitness; others sought to keep the continual ritual because of *habit*; still others were in the gym to meet other people, or maybe to find a brief-sexual-*encounter*.

After this rejuvenating work-out in which Jana exceeded her planned time and extended it to 43 minutes!, she headed to the Jacuzzi for some relaxation.

The Jacuzzi was in the basement-level and she took the stairs down.

The Jacuzzi was empty-of-people...operating as if it were with people...spewing energy to the air around.

After a brief shower Jana entered the Jacuzzi... slowly submerging herself up to her neck.

Jana **IMAGINED** (created) being in a natural setting: somewhere in a tropical paradise filled with wild-men-of-*passion*.

Jana then fantasized about ONE-DAY finding

the perfect man: a man that could sweep-her-

off her feet *and-into* a-blissful-relationship of-love-and-*passion*.

p a s s i o n !

Suddenly Jana heard a voice,

"Hi!"

....a voice too loud to be her day dream.

"Hi!" the voice came again.

Jana opened her eyes and there stood a beautiful man in his early thirties: dark skinned with light blonde hair that curled at the *end*s.

This man was evidently fit (possessing an inviting muscular demeanor).

Jana lifted herself up from a squatted position and sat down inside the Jacuzzi.

This man came down the water to join her.

"My name is Joey. What's yours?"

"Jana"

"Do you come her often Jana?"

"Not often"

The man did not say another word: he neared his body next to hers. He stood face to face with Jana.

Joey caressed his chest against Jana's breasts.

Jana did not stop him.

She did not comprehend what was happening to her.

Instead of attempting to figure it out, Jana took it in and enjoyed it...

...enjoying every *moment* of it...savoring the flesh in front of her...

...allowing some sort of therapy to take place...to unfold!

This Joey was handsome: his blue eyes were *sooth*ing to Jana's eyes.

Jana felt him underneath the water as he touched her thighs with his hands:

...strolling his hands back and forth from her hips to her knees...creating strong sexual sensations within Jana that began to grow!

Jana just sat there motionless...

...allowing everything to continue...

...not resisting but wanting more!

Jana closed her eyes and suddenly felt his lips caress hers.

Joey had *a wonderful* warmth on his lips.

Jana opened her mouth and received his tongue into hers.

Jana caressed her tongue with Joey's...

...both beings savoring the movements of one-another *intertwining*.

Joey, as the man called himself, then reached between Jana's legs with his fingers...

...moving Jana's bikini and going underneath it...*caressing* her clitoris gently in a circular motion.

Jana moaned.

After 2 minutes of slow blissful pleasure, Joey penetrated her vagina with his two fingers...index and middle fingers...

...elegantly stroking inwards and outwards...

...causing Jana to let out a loud M O A N.

The action provoked Jana to reach out to his shorts and grasped them on the sides.

Jana pulled them down and then reached for this man's penis...

... taking possession of his large sexual muscle with both hands.

Jana stroked it back and forth: from the tip to his `pel-vis` (from where it grew from).

After massaging it for seven-minutes, Joey lifted her out of the Jacuzzi and onto the cement floor...gently laying her down.

Joey then removed Jana's lower bikini and then opened her legs apart while squatting down as she simultaneously grabbed his penis and guided it to her vagina...

Joey was coming in for the Landing!

Jana felt the penetration as a strong thrust!

The man kept it in for a while (taking-in-her-tightness-and-wetness)...he then started a hip-motion-of-back-and-forth....

...back-and-forth-back-and-forth...

Jana was climaxing TOO-soon and wanted more "faster faster faster!" Jana yelled.

Joey sensed her climaxing and thrusted his penis into her faster-and-**deeper**-faster-and-**deeper**-faster-and-**deeper***!*

Jana moaned and moaned and ***spurt out*** a LOUD yell. Jana had come and Joey continued till he climaxed on top of her belly...

...releasing all of his precious *gooo* on to her!...

Jana grabbed his penis with her hands and stroked it until all-the-sperm that wanted to come out **CAME-*ONTO-HER!***

Jana stood up and kissed Joey long and passionately and then laid back down..

... motionless and tired...

... motionless and tired...

...slowly closing her *eyes*.

...after a good 5 minutes that seemed 50, Jana opened them:

Jana was in the Jacuzzi alone with her index-finger and middle-finger thrust inside her vagina.

It had all been a DREAM!

It felt so so so real, so real!

"How could it be **not real**?" she thought. "What the *hell*!?" Jana thought.

Jana could not find `reason` in her consciousness.

Was she asleep or was she awake?

Was she asleep or was she awake?

"Am I asleep or am I awake?".

"Am I asleep or am I awake?".

Jana desperately needed a man...

.... a man who would love her and please her when she felt the urge to thrust-her-emotions through the pleasures-of-orgasm.

Jana *realize*d that maybe she had been TOO picky and not-letting-men-in who made offers to her for a relationship.

Jana was too complex in her choosing:

1) He had to be a certain body type

2) A certain hair color

3) A certain skin color

4) A particular birth sign

5) Someone witty-enough who would amuse her during long evenings.

And the list went on on on and on!

Jana was looking for happiness:

Yet maybe she first needed to find and accept her independent self-happiness...

...and allow her **repressed-***Flamboyancy* in herself first to flourish?!

TOFLOURISH *!*

Maybe, when it came to choosing a man, Jāna needed to learn to make others laugh and feel comfortable first. Jana was usually the domineering type who wanted it her way or the highway. [Oh my J!...not good J not good!]

Despite the sudden desire to change herself...

...Jana often avoided the topic of true self-analysis and moved on to other things away from her person (like most humans!)...

As a consequence: Jana did not allow herself to **TRULY** change.

Was this the way the human-being-is-*made*?:

... Resisting change at every cost!?...

...Not realizing that a rigid ways of thinking leads to **pains** **pains** and **MORE** ***pains!***

Or was **this rigidity** a consequence of modern society acculturating the human being to-be SELFISH?

[Good question.]

Jana removed her hand from her groin and slipped the small cloth that covered her under-privates back into its *intended* position.

Jana slowly stood up.

No one was around.

At that late hour, the pool area was *completely* empty...

EXCEPT for a tiny security-camera **spying into the room***!*

This invasion of privacy didn't matter to Jana at that moment: what mattered to Jana at that *very-moment* was that she was feeling *very-at-ease* and nothing seemed to bother her

...not at that moment...

...not at that moment...

...no no no...

...not at that PRECISE moment!

The orgasm numbed her mind and her body at that instance...this is what Jana needed and this is what Jana received!

Jana had denied the orgasm for so long...

...allowing **other bodiless-beings** to PERTURB her peace **instead**!

The carbon body that all the beings of this world are encased-in makes it difficult to find true paths.

TRUE PATHS

...especially when *blind*ed by all the distractions-of-this-**realm**.

Jana proceeded to walk to the lockers to shower and dress.

Jana was con*tent*...

... (even if only for THAT MOMENT!).

Chapter Four
Struggle and Discovery

When Jana returned to her apartment from the gym everything was quiet. It was two thirty two in the morning when she entered and closed her apartment's main door behind her. Jana needed sleep, yet she did not want to sleep.

Jana's mind was conflicting again as to wanting a true change in her life.

The struggle kept her occupied.

Jana thought, "maybe I need to…"… she did not finish her sentence when suddenly her cat jumped at her for affection.

Jana became distracted and decided that it was best just to sleep it off and feel better in the morning.

As she lay in bed Jana started thinking about school.

School was scheduled to start on Moonday…so Jana had time to sort the items in her classroom before the students arrived.

And even though Jana had her lesson plans complete and her teaching visual materials in order, she took the time to evaluate her plans...always seeking to make them better or to tailor them to the specific type of students she would encounter for the new school year: students who were either visual, audio, or kinesthetic learners (or a combination of all three).

Jana usually examined each student's academic records to determine what learning styles worked best for them. This helped her constructively modify her lessons accordingly for creating the most effective, conducive learning environment for her students. Jana had to do this for each of her five period sessions. Each period consisted of between 34 to 43 students! So that was between 170 to 215 students!

Jana also had to go to faculty meetings during these preparation days to hear the same jargon of every year!

This year the school would have a new principal.

This was the *six*th principal in *six* years!

Six years!

"Something must be going on *upstairs*!" Jana thought.

"It's not my concern: this week I'll just focus on my preparations to teach Spanish this new school year as always".

Jana *closed* her eyes and *fell asleep.*

Jana had not taken off her clothes or shoes. She just lay there in bed, peacefully; if only for a while.

Jana began to see visions in her dreams:

She was riding a *white* horse. It was a *white* stallion.

white!

A gust of wind pulled her hair. Jana enjoyed the cool breeze run through her face.

Jana felt free!

free !

Jana was on an open grassy plain riding her horse in freedom.

There were no buildings or houses it was just the plains, her horse, and herself.

After a fierce gallop toward the *east*, Jana saw some teepees. As she neared them within 52 meters, she began to lead herself innerly to this community of nomads; of naturalists; of warriors; of freedom fighters.

Jana felt at home as she approached: a feeling she had never-felt-in-her-wake-times.

Jana came upon a man: a very strong man: six feet seven...bearing dark skin and a determined stare.

Jana had never seen this man yet she felt a sudden impulse-of-knowing-him.

"Tlatla Fa Pa Sae" he spoke...his voice deep with sorrow.

Jana stood in front of him....staring into his eyes.... not knowing completely.....yet knowing something of what he said.

"Things are changing."

Although her consciousness didn't know... deep-down-in-her-unconsciousness Jana understood.... yet didn't attempt to translate the complete meaning in her mind.

A pulsating sound began to develop. It kept getting louder and louder.

Everything began to disappear around Jana...

The pulsing sound was her annoying-alarm-clock that kept on *roaring* in the room.

Jana opened her eyes and saw the wooden ceiling with its wooden beams stream across vertically.

Jana leaped out of bed (half asleep) and turned off the annoying sound.

Jana stood there motionless: thinking.

Thinking!

"What was this dream meant to tell me?"

Jana pondered this question understanding she had never ridden a horse before...

Thinking!

Jana proceeded to the shower and took a quick dip. She rushed out of the shower, more or less toweled dried herself, and put on her denim jeans (without underwear), her baby blue blouse with *white* flowers (without a bra), and finally her light gray Arabic-running-shoes (without socks).

Without!

Chapter Five
Work and Opportunity

It was now Mercury Day the 12th of September 2007, the second day of work; although the kids were not scheduled to begin school until *Moon*day.

The administration had given her and the others *six* days to get ready before the *commotion* of teens!

When Jana arrived at the private preparatory college high school in West Los Angeles, she *pull*ed up to the driveway of the staff parking.

Jana found a spot and moved into it: being careful not to hit another car. Last school year Jana had dented one of the cars as she *pull*ed into a spot.

As she walked out of her car, Jana decided not to sign in and just head straight to her classroom.

Going up the stairs of the main 2nd story building, Jana arrived to her room: room number 232.

Once at the door, Jana reached for her keys and then puzzled through the batch of *linked keys*.

She could not find the classroom key!

Jana quickly remembered that yesterday the *doors* were all *open* to all of the classrooms since new locks were being replaced and *no keys* were yet available.

Her actual possession of her classroom key was back three months ago on June 19, 2007, when Jana had *submit*ted them to the office for replacements.

Jana was *forced* to go *downstairs* and retrieve the new classroom key.

As Jana headed toward the office, walking through the second-floor corridor, a voice called out from a door left open.

"Jana, hi, how are you doing?"

Jana was caught by surprise.

It was Mr. Brown (Matt Brown). He was a young mathematics teacher who had come aboard last year: fresh out of graduate school.

Matt was **27** years old... a white Anglo-Saxon male with light blue eyes, blond hair, and a smile that enthralled anyone to him who received a glimpse of it!

Matt had asked Jana out on a date last *September* when the prior school year had started. Jana had refused because Matt seemed shallow in the way he carried himself; and because he was much younger than she.

Jana felt at the time that he would dump her eventually for a younger, more attractive woman. So Jana decided to stay away from him: despite Matt being handsome, a **6** feet 1 inch tall male with enormous hands-and-feet.

No-doubt-about-it:

Matt's smile was *golden*: but Jana had to *resist*.

Besides, Jana couldn't involve herself with someone at work. If they would ever break up, Jana would have to see him every day at work...which would make her life even more *difficult*!

"Hi Matt," Jana said leaning back from the outside of the door.

 "Hey Jen, I was *wondering* if maybe you had a change of heart.. and would be willing to go out with me this time".

Matt smiled.

Jana looked at him *intently*: *trying to remember* what she had told herself before.

Awe... there it was... the information:

"Sorry Matt, I'm not interested. You are a very handsome man, I'm sure you will have no problem finding a beautiful young girl your age."

Jana did not want his company.

She didn't want to get hurt; or maybe Jana was genuinely not interested at any level.

Jana did *not quite know* how to interpret the mixed-messages within herself.

"*Listen* Jana, you are a beautiful woman. I know you are slightly older than me; but age doesn't matter to me...whether I am with a young woman or someone older than my years...it doesn't matter."

"I just want to get to know you better. You seem to have that *special-thing* about you that draws me to you."

Jana looked at Matt more intently and inclined her face slightly... making a smile and a pause, and then she said intriguingly:

 "What do you mean '*special thing*'?"

"Well Jana, what I mean is that it seems you have that inner spark that radiates from you. You always seem to be in deep thought... and that attracts me to you."

Jana looked at Matt for a second; then looked at the ground for a moment... *scanning* the ground for about 3 seconds and then looked up to his *eyes* again for about 3 more seconds... and then said:

"Okay".

Matt made a surprised look. "Okay?!... Great!"

Jana needed a change-in-her-life; she needed to find a-different-way-of-thinking; Jana needed *company*; she needed to-get-out-of-herself: to-find-peace; to-find-growth; to-find-maturity.

"We'll talk later Matt, I got to get my keys. Here's my telephone number." Jana *reach*ed for her purse, pulled out a pen and an old receipt from the market, and wrote: 310-399-6767. She handed it to Matt, smiled, and walked out.

The day at work went well.

Jana organized her lesson materials, ran copies, placed each text book under each desk (a-classroom-copy): the students would be assigned another one to take home.

Jana had also decorated the walls with cultural Hispanic scenes. A lot of them were pictures from Mexico City and Barcelona. Additionally, she had some other posters demonstrating samples of conjugations from a *root* verb to its changes in form as to person and number and gender.

G E N-DER

Jana gave some of the posters a final touch-up by adding colored streamers around them (along with adding cultural hats from different *parts* of Mexico and other Latin American countries).

Jana felt satisfied with a good day's work of preparation for the new school year.

Jana always tried to make her class as inviting as possible in order to keep the students entertained and focused with the subject at hand:

E s pa ñ o l

Español

Jana had been teaching Spanish for quite a while and consequently *accumulated* a good number of items for her room; in addition to having innovative and tailored pedagogical *systems* to keep the students focused.

The teaching profession was a good *distraction* for Jana for so many years: yet something inside her was empty and she needed to fill this ~~VOID~~.

Jana wasn't sure what this ~~VOID~~ was.

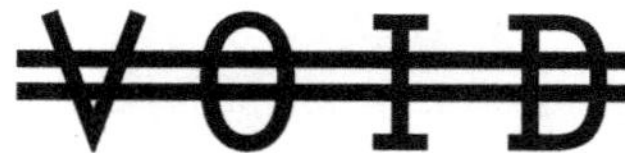

Jana needed to do some exploring: let her mind

wander wander wander...

... in order to find it!

FIND IT!

Jana locked her room and headed out to the parking lot. She noticed that Matt's door was still open. Jana didn't feel like saying goodbye lest she may disturb his preparations; although Jana did feel an urge to say bye.

conflicted Jana Was!

What would happen if Jana let him into her life?

She would have a man in her life on a regular basis again!

Yet, Jana didn't know Matt...so that spelled:

C a u tion.

Jana had *learned* that people put personality fronts at work (in order to conform to societal expectations, I guess).

People usually act different out-of-the work-*environment*...many times even drastically different!

I kid you not!!!

Chapter Six
Jana and Her Past Lovers

As Jana drove out of the parking lot, she began to amuse herself over fantasies with Matt. How would it be to have him in bed? How would he perform? Would he last or come fast?

Jana began to *contemplate* the human-male-*species*.

She had learned that at first most men come fast the first time and then longer the *second* and *third* time: all within the *same* session!

Jana also learned that a man lasted longer as their relationship became regular.

Why was this so?...Jana continued to contemplate.

Tentatively Jana concluded, somewhat negatively, that it was maybe because the thrill of having sex with the *same* person would dissipate the flair-of-passion the more times sex became regular...

...no more urgency to conquer and divide!

s a m e

l a m e

C a i n !

Or maybe, she thought, it was because men naturally lose *interest* in their partner.

Jana liked to *believe* that maybe they lasted longer because of love.

As Jana turned into her favorite **café KKanaKoluKKūMāhā** location...she began to analyze herself about this topic:

How good was SHE in bed for a man?

From her prior experience, Jana had come to realize that men like lots-of-movements and positions. They also like experimenting...but experimenting with a flow of rhythmic-and-pulsating movements.

Jana rated herself at the middle of the sexually competent scale: plenty-of-room-for-improvement!

She did move with different motions of rhythm: giving the man pleasure; yet she lacked the skill to move with quick and surprising strokes…some of which she had never known about first hand.

Jana learned about these movement techniques in books she briefly read in sex-improvement-books that she occasionally glanced-at in her local book store.

Jana wouldn't dare buy such a book in person...choosing instead to exam such books on the spot at the bookstore.

The good news is that now with the advent of the high-use-of-the-Internet: Jana was considering ordering one of these books Online in the privacy of her own home!

Digging further into this topic, Jana realized with a heightened-awareness that she lacked that sudden-flow-of-movement to create a chaos of pleasure for a man.

"Well", she thought, "at least I've gotten better since the *beginning*!"

This *beginning* commenced during Jana's freshman year in college when she began having sex with her boyfriend Greg.

Sex-*Beginning*-Awareness

During those times, Jana would just lay on her back, open her legs, and let Greg thrust himself into her.

Jana had never once (during that time) been on top.

At that beginning Jana didn't know that she could have asked for a compromise-of-positions in order to help her feel-feel-feel!

Being on top: Jana could have had control of the motions-and-depthness of his penetration...

...permitting her to also feel the excitement of-the-pressing of her clitoris against his pubis (The Superior *Ram*us of Pubis)...

...providing her with true-sexual-pleasure along with a sense of control in the act-of-sexual-intercourse.

[Gentlemen take note! Learn how to please a woman!:)]

[RAM: the sacred animal of the people who Rule this World!]

Greg was not a great performer in bed; Jana seldom came during the numerous times he came throughout her relationship with him.

Jana did however enjoy holding him as-he-slept.

Jana enjoyed feeling his presence near her. She felt protected having a man in bed with her. Jana felt she wasn't alone; although she found herself mostly alone in-her-*thoughts*.

...alone in-her-*thoughts*.

*Unfortunate*ly, Jana felt disconnected in that relationship. She didn't find her "soul-mate" in Greg.

Gregory
Gregorious!

A misnomer for the person Jana had met.

Far from being alert or *watch*ful as the name implies!

a **BEAST!** Greg was!

Jana was naive in those days...not being able to adequately dissect a *human psyche*!

Well, Jana is still naïve...but less in the present!

What Jana did find in Greg was a man-boy consumed with his school work, his economics classes. A man-boy who rarely exercised. That is probably why he came so fast most of the time...within $2^{.5}$ minutes!

And no: Greg did not warm up in preparation for the act of sexual intercourse...the **beast** simply went full throttle and then fell asleep!

[¡Qué pendejo!]

Greg was *6* feet *2* inches tall and over weight: weighing about *270* pounds. His fat was mostly flab on his belly and hip.

Maybe if Greg had exercised regularly he would not have only lost the weight but last longer as he penetrated Jana...and pleasing her as well instead of just himself.

egoísta

自分勝手

zelfzuchtig

bencil

Jana also remembered how worrisome of a person Greg was: always tense in how he would muster enough money to pay his quarterly tuition.

Greg's parents did not have any money and he refused to take out student loans; knowing that he would have to eventually pay a loan institution and find himself indebted after college.

In his *mind,* Greg didn't want to be an immediate post-college servant to the masters.

Yet that is exactly what the *system* produces!

Jana tried to help Greg with his worriedness-proneness by placing love massages on his shoulder as he studied.

"Stop that Jana, not now!"

Other times she would make dinner for both of them despite having her own examinations the n*ext* day!

Greg just ate and went *back* to work...he did not even say "Thank you!".

Two minds viewing life through different *lenses*.

How did this couple come to be?

Good question.

During those times Jana felt *reject*ed.

[Obviously!:(...who wouldn't!]

Sure there were lots of offers from other guys: begging her to allow them to court her on a regular basis.

But Jana was a loyalist: she was *devoted* completely to the *man* she was with and would not allow other possibilities; possibilities that *may* have included finding someone who wasn't so *consume*d with his work and his own selfish needs!

Something Sort-Of-Broke that loyalty!

One time, at the college locker room, as Jana finished her shower and was preparing to dress after soccer practice with the university's girl's soccer team, Jana encountered a sexual advance on her by a fellow team player.

The aggressive team player was a husky girl seven inches taller than Jana; a whale of an Anglo-Saxon woman, weighing at least 250 pounds, who always looked at Jana differently.

Jana did not understand.

[*Naïve* I guess.]

 On the field this husky girl was intimidating!

This husky fellow team player named **Jennifer** looked more like a defensive-line-male-football player than a female soccer player!

Despite her weight Jennifer was fast and a trickster at snatching the ball! That's probably why she made the team!

As they *shower*ed, Jennifer would always stare at Jana, devouring her, it seemed to Jana, with her eyes.

This husky girl's name of Jennifer did not quite fit her. Literally, she looked like a man! Big John! John seemed more appropriate for this Beast!

Jennifer was obviously overweight but had a lot of power-and-endurance for such a large person.

Big John was obviously physically fit yet you couldn't tell by *look*ing at her.

The keen skills Big John had *acquire*d somewhere was noticeable!

Jennifer played rough on the field and didn't talk much to anyone.

Big John seemed anti-social (not shy: jut not interested in small talk).

Jennifer kept to herself most of the *time* except when she YELLED at the other teammates for not performing well during a planned play.

Big John was a strategist...

... and every minute-move meant something to her.

So when the girls *detour*ed from the plan or an improvised variation of the plan, Jennifer would get

so so SO **upseT**

The other girls were afraid of Big John...and tried very hard not to cross her in anyway.

Even the coach was intimidated!

On that day in the the locker-room, Jennifer's sexual advancement toward Jana came sudden and unexpected.

While Jana was dressing after her shower, Jennifer violently grabbed Jana by the arm.

Before Jana could protest: Jennifer *ram*med her body against Jana's...pushing Jana against the metal lockers...this winded Jana.

Jana was about to attempt to form some vocalization when Big John placed her mouth on Jana's: not allowing her to talk.

The *ram*ming had left Jana without breath and Jana was struggling to breathe through her nostrils.

This was followed by a swift-swipe to Jana's panties: tearing them from her body.

Jana tried helplessly to stop this, but Jennifer persisted: she was too-strong for Jana.

Big JOHN pushed Jana more against the lockers and pressed her huge, large breasts against Jana's.

The continual *ram*ming was becoming unbearable.

Jana looked at Jennifer's eyes and tried to plead with her-stare to stop: but it was all in vain.

Jennifer had *plan*ned this!

No one was around: everyone had left.

Jana was trapped*!*

With her lips on Jana, Big John again swiped her large hand in-between Jana's legs: this time penetrating her with two of her fingers (the 4-finger...and the taller one next to it....its accomplice!).

Jennifer began to stoke Jana's vagina.

Jana tried to move away: but the more she tried the more Jennifer *push*ed her *against* the lockers: causing Jana excruciating pain.

The stroking persisted so violently that Jana was left with no choice but to give into Jennifer.

Every stroke into Jana's vagina just made Jana weaker in resisting.

Big John knew this.

Every stroke began to arouse Jana so much that Jana could not resist but *to-begin* TO-FIND *pleasure*-in-her-violation.

Jana became CONFUSED as to this change in mindset.

This ***sexual-intoxication*** made Jana completely vulnerable to her ***sexual-nature***.

The Giant had forced Jana to-*Delve* into a ***trance-of-sexual-ecstasy***.

As this aggression continued: Jana's hormones *TRANSFORMED HER INTO* Jana-Sex-Goddess-of Pleasure-and-Emanating Pleasure.

[Involuntarily I make a point to add!]

With this transformation, Jana looked into Jennifer's eyes for the first time in a *deliberate*-wanting-way.

Jana began to *violent*ly kiss Jennifer and began to probe-her-tongue-into-hers.

Jana's arms began trying to reach the enormous girth of Jennifer's huge **ASS**....

....She gripped what she could...pulsating in pleasure with every stroke Jennifer made into her groin.

After ten minutes: Jana began to sweat!

When Jennifer had seen that Jana had been aroused to the point of no return...

...The Giant female gently placed Jana onto the bleacher.

Jennifer the Giant Agressor then spread Jana's legs wide open, bent down, holding her legs from stretching to far apart with her upper arms, and

sank-her-mouth into Jana's vagina.

Jana moaned with pleasure: she could feel Jennifer's tongue probing her outer vagina, and then followed by a sinking of her *long-tongue* into Jana's vagina.

Jana was not able to make sense out of **anything** anymore.

Anything Anymore

Anything!

At that moment, for Jana, Jennifer did not represent a woman to her **anymore**.

With every pleasure-*splurge*, Jana began to see **GIANT JENNIFER** as a man.

[And Indeed Jennifer Looked and Behaved Like A Man!]

The sensation on Jana's clitoris began to intensify more and more as Jennifer's whole face was on Jana's groin.

Jana began to moan and yell with pleasure: Jana was coming and **coming-strong**!

Suddenly, at the point of Jana's orgasm, Jennifer **STOPPED!**

Big John John lifted herself up from a somewhat kneeling-squatting position and took what little clothes she-the GIANT had off (which was only the Giant's panties).

(Giant John-Jennifer literary TORE her panties off of herself!)

Jana understood immediately what Jennifer wanted her to do.

As Jennifer placed her enormous body onto the other bleacher next to her... the Giant pulled Jana to her.

....not letting go of her prey!

Jana went down on Jennifer... fervorously licking her ENORMOUS vagina ferociously!

Jana had lost all inhibitions: Big John-Jennifer had left Jana wanting more.

The Enormous Giant grabbed Jana's hair and shoved her closer to her, giving the Giant a

climatic ecstasy of thr**O**bbing-thrills.

thr**O**bbing-thrills

At that moment, Giant John-Jennifer gave

a long long **HUGE** m**O**an

followed by a **scream** as the Giant Female cli**T**maxed into a HUGE-**con**vulsive-

O rg*asm.*

When it was *clear* that Jennifer had come (a Stranded-Whale-Of-A-Site!): Jana sat up, went over Jennifer's enormous thorax, and kissed Jennifer on the lips...ready to part ways with the beast.

Giant John-Jennifer, however, ever knowing Jana had not climaxed (as the Giant had purposefully delayed Jana's automatic-biological explosion): began kissing Jana.

At that very moment, the Beast lowered her *left* hand and grabbed Jana's clitoris and began stroking it and periodically sinking her FAT-long-fingers into Jana's vagina.

Using her Right claw, the Beast firmly held Jana's *aass*... still maintaining physical-*control* over Jana.

Jana began losing self-control once more!: Jana lowered herself slightly and began to fervorously suck on Jennifer's GIANT nipples.

As each clitor*octic*-stroke increased **momentum-velocity** onto the captive: Jana began to moan.

...first softly and then less softly and then even less softly...

and finally

loudly more loudly and even more **loudly***!*

What followed was an uncontrollable **scream** coming from Jana as her whole body

shiVered rapidly....creating **quantic**-needles-of-**freezing-points**!

The *endless-looking*-microdots were *visible* on Jana's ENTIRE BODY....even her back!

And this Time Finally, after COMPLETE LOST of any control: Jana clasped Jennifer's shoulders with all her *might*, shot her head up toward the ceiling in ecstasy: giving a LONG-AND-STRENUOUS-moan and **yell**.

Jana had climaxed as never before!...at the hands of a **Female** *Beast*!

After the beast cuddled her for a few minutes, it released its prey!!!

The *prey* slowly limply and painfully-slowly limply put on her clothes, then grabbed her gym bag, and then walked out of the gym with sweaty hands, feet, head, and *whole body*!

Jana never returned to the soccer team.

In fact, Jana never ever ever neared that area again.

Jana kept a low profile for the rest of her college stay...only *going* to class and then leaving campus right *away*.

Jana had a trauma that seemed unreconcilable un comprehensible un healing un un un.

Jana never reported the

RAPE!

Chapter Seven
Jana's Parents

Back to her present reality, Jana was waiting in line to buy coffee at a nearby **café KKanaKoluKKūMāhā** after her work on 12th of *September* 2007.

It appeared to Jana that being alone was driving her *crazy*...a strong desire to turn to someone for comfort and companionship was growing on her.

Although such a strong sense of urgency never moved Jana to the point of being uneasy: now was not the case.

Jana was beginning to come to the conclusion that being *a loner* was not in her best interest. Jana had to open up and allow people to fill her life.

Her mother was in Oklahoma: *busy* with her new relationship of which Jana knew nothing about: both mother and daughter really didn't share any lasting relationship up to the present: Jana felt alienated.

 Jana's mother always seemed distant with her.

Maybe Jana's mother resented that Jana was the daughter of the love-of-her-life that had left her?

Jana's father was a *Wild Stallion* who was not easily tamed: he was an adventurer from a dysfunctional family in an Indian reservation in Oklahoma.

Jana's father was brought up in poverty and lost encouragement...something that comes with living poor within a BADLY-CREATED reservation (and being shunned outside of it by the newly created world!).

...but Jana's father's "distancing" mentality must have also been irritated by something **"deeper"**...

....something Jana knew nothing about.

...Jana refused to place blame on her parents.

...for all they ever showed her when they were "calm"...was LOVE.

Wild Feather, as Jana's father was called, grew up with a mother who was a drunk; his father, *Red* Feather, was *kill*ed in an accidental boar hunting expedition when he was only two years old.

From this incident, it seemed that Jana's paternal grandmother grew into a bitter wo*man* who was not able to replace the man she loved so dearly; a man who cared for her-every-need.

The widow found men at the reservation: but most of them just opted to live *off* government subsidies.

Wild Feather's mother wanted a real man...but did not find him. Maybe she did not know how to look for the right man after the death of her husband.

(The *old-ways* had been replaced by *corrupt impositions* of the new rulers of the land.)

So instead: the widow's son (Jana's father "Wild Feather") as a *child* was introduced to various *men* who *came and went.*

came and went.

came

                                        and went.

Wild Feather had no real example of what a
decent man of the house was like:

...his examples were men that would beat him if
he did not bring them their beer or do special
favors he resented doing.

                    Special Favors
Special Favors

                                    Special Favors

The only lasting thing Wild Feather learned were
examples of men who were mischievous and
conspicuous in demonstrating their vices....

...Men that came in and out of his mother's house
as if it were a WHORE HOUSE.

                    *Wh**OO**re h**O**use*

                    *Wh**OO**re h**O**use*

Because of these childhood *traumas*: Wild Feather **psychologically** was not capable [no I don't wish to place 'incapable'] of settling down for long periods of time: although initially he made an effort.

The deep resentments that he had **With**in-h**im** did not allow him to accept the love that Jana's Mother (Doris) was providing him on a long term basis.

Although this was different in the beginning as Wild Feather fervently received unconditional love from Doris.

Wild Feather truly tried to be different.

He appeared to be a *lost soul* with-a-past that would-not leave him alone.

After he had brought his family to the reservation (at the recommendation of his wife Doris) things were hopeful.

Doris had thought that after the baby was born that it would be a good idea to move to the reservation to help Wild Feather bring closure-to-his-past.

Unfortunately that plan BACK-FIRED!

Moving back began giving her husband wild-flushes of terrible sleepless nights and something kept nagging at the inside-back of his head which Wild Feather SHARED-WITH-NO-ONE.

After he parted ways from his family: Wild Feather did attempt to continue to see his daughter on a *daily* basis on this reservation.

In fact, they *spent* long-walks talking about the adventures told to him by his uncles of his father's hunting expeditions.

Wild Feather also took the time to swing Jana on a swing he built in front of her house.

Jana loved her father and was heart*broken* when her mother decided to move out of the reservation and back into the *city*.

This, of course, made it difficult for her to see her father often.

Doris had waited long *enough!*...

...enough hoping that Wild Feather would come back to her.

Enough!

For her own sanity, Doris had to make the decision to move on and move-*out* of his range-of-presence.

Wild Feather would come once a month to visit Jana in Tulsa, Oklahoma.

Unfortunately: all of that stopped suddenly when she reached seven-years-old.

At that young age: Jana's mother decided to relocate from Tulsa to Muskogee, Oklahoma...seeking something different than *Painful-Pasts*.

Jana missed her father and could not understand why he stopped visiting her.

As a teenager, one of Jana's teenage friends offered to drive her to the reservation to look for her father.

After inquiring with her uncle (Wild Feather's cousin): Jana did not get anywhere.

Uncle Humphrey told her that Wild Feather had *stop*ped *coming* around his house suddenly.

Humphrey searched for him and did not find him.

Jana was heartbroken.

[Guess he didn't search long enough!: like **most people**]

Doris then moved Jana to a middle-class Muscogee neighborhood on a nurse's salary.

Doris had gone back to school and received her license as a registered nurse.

Doris worked long hours and was out most nights.

Consequently, little time was spent with Jana.

Jana concluded later on in her life that peace did not live within her mother...

...she could not sleep and so she found an *"escape"*...

... in a job where she did not have to spend the night.

Jana often had a sitter during the nights.

Both of Jana's maternal grandparents were *kill*ed in an automobile accident when Doris was twelve.

Doris was (somewhat!) brought up by her aunt Betsy who did not provide that motherly love that Doris so desperately sought.

Doris missed both her parents.

In her being this Irish-orphan had an-emptiness inside her that she had-hoped could be fulfilled by a man:

... in her case:

Wild Feather.

Doris had met Wild Feather at a *Circle K* when she was just seventeen. In him, it soothed her to be with someone that appeared to love her. The relationship worked for several years but came crashing down when they married and moved to the reservation.

Wild Feather changed in that reservation and stopped being the loving man he was at first: "Why did he become like that?", Doris would *think*. She went through many pains seeing Wild

Feather **sl*ip* a way** *f r o m h* e r.

Doris often cried in silence in the bathroom to the point that she would sleep in the tub trying to forget her pain; her turmoil.

When Doris returned to the city with her daughter: she did not create new friends or sought **a new** *love*.

...her mind was still *devoted* to him.

Doris did not announce her return to her Aunt Betsy since this reluctant guardian never seemed to really care about her. Consequently, apart from her mother, Jana found herself UTTERLY alone.

As a result, Jana, through her mother's example, became a loner with no real life.

Both felt unequivocally alone: with no human to move them toward a direction of happiness.

'QUIVOCALLY-*UN*

QUIVOCALLY-*UN*

QUIVOCALLY-*UN*

[Dependency in a human is Never a sound mindset!]

After some flings in high school, Jana did not find any stability in terms of a relationship.

Greg from college had *dump*ed her for a classmate he had met in his Physics class: these two new LOVE−BIRDS shared all the things in common in terms of interest in the *physical* phenomenon of this physical existence...but nothing more.

Self-Centeredness Was Their Bridge!

This *dump*ing left Jana feeling incompetent and worthless.

During that time, Jana felt no value in herself worthy to give to another human being: she had become even more *psychological*ly sca**rred** and could not recover at that moment to allow herself to build a healthy normal relationship with another *human.*

Jana unconsciously had developed insecurity and trust issues that she was not aware of having at that time in her consciousness.

This young woman was in denial as to the root cause of something she did not know how to properly evaluate. Consequently, Jana let these negative inner-workings linger behind her light's eyes!

It would take some time for her to snap out of her *rigid-frame-of-mind!*

Jana's condition imposed on her by her **human-***encased-form* made it difficult to *remember* who she really was in terms of eternity!

An *Eternal Being* We ALL are!

Eternal Being

Eternal Being

No one knew Jana was a loner.

When Greg broke up with her, Jana's acquaintances *assume*d that she had found someone else.

Jana lived a lie-of-a-life!: perpetuated by her saying she was going to *meet* so and so at so and so *time*.

Her true life-experience at that moment was just her straight forward focus on her professional work.

After work she would mostly *drown* herself in movies and food.

Movies And Food

Movies And Food!

Since Jana was young and had a fast *meta*bolism, she did not gain weight as others probably would have by the consumption she was taking in with little or no exercise.

meta

meta

Inside of Jana she fell deep in

M UD.

...feeling no outlet from the *confinements* of her past.

Chapter Eight
Jana Meets Miguel

As Jana was thinking of this difficult break up with Greg on the 12th of September 2007, waiting in line inside **café KKanaKoluKKūMāhā** after work, she had zoned out from her present.

A voice came at her but she did not perceive it:

"Mam, can I take your order?"

"Mam, can I take your order?" repeated the worker behind the pastries.

Apparently he had been asking her for some time.

Jana did not see or hear the worker....she was completely off in her thoughts.

It was not uncommon for Jana to go off on one of her day dreams or deep thoughts on something that caught her attention. Although when she was teaching, she was completely there...immersed in her profession. Out of her profession though, Jana wandered frequently in her mind.

"Señorita, would you like to order?" a voice came from-behind-her.

That voice caught her attention and brought her back to the present.

"Oh, yea, let me have a decaf mocha please!".

The voice behind her again began to utter words:

"Are you all right Señorita?".

Jana was not "all right"!

She was alone.

She thought, "I don't want to hook up with someone just because I'm alone; just because I need a man in my life."

Jana again returned into deep thought and was thinking in her mind:

"Matt at work has pursued me for quite some time: but I really don't feel anything for him?"

" I don't love him and I don't think I can. I don't feel that certain chemistry between us or at least not coming from me!"

Perplexed She Was!

"I don't feel that certain feeling that excites me... like that feeling I had with Greg....even though he was a complete idiot!"

"Despite being an idiot and me accepting it: Everything was going so well with him."

"I would cook for him when he came home; I would clean for him; I would make love to him when he requested it. I was in love with Greg and he left me for a younger woman; a full bred Caucasian woman!"

"Oh Greg, why did you leave me? Didn't you see how much I needed you?...how much I pleaded with you to stay with me? You left me alone after being together for so many years!"

" Greg come back to me! Greg!" Jana was aching inside as she impatiently recited these words in her mind.

[It had not been the first time she had said them!]

"Hi, what is your name?" the voice with an accent continued from behind her.

This voice brought her back again to the present.

Jana responded as she began turning around:

"I'm sorry to ignore you but I was…"

Jana FROZE.

Behind her was a man that caught her attention immediately after she saw him.

He was *Beautiful*!

"Hi, my name is Miguel: pleasure to meet you!"

"Are you all right?"

Jana could not speak.

She looked into Miguel's eyes and instantly felt that connection.

That connection!

C-O-N-N-E-C-TION!

"Well, it is a beautiful day, isn't it?"

Miguel waited to get some verbal response from Jana.

None came.

Jana just stood there and looked into his eyes.

Her stomach began with butterflies... and then a pulsating rhythm began within her whole body.

To her Miguel was *Beautiful*.

Beautiful!

A man with large caramel eyes that radiated peacefulness to Jana.

Jana was unable to move her-fascination away from Miguel's eyes.

She was in a *trance*.

Jana forced herself to snap out of it!

She regained control!

CONTROL!

"Yes yes thank you. I am fine."

After Miguel requested and received his beverage Jana said:

"Do you want to sit together?"

Miguel smiled and responded:

"Yes!"

Both spoke for quite a while about how beautiful the day was and how much they both loved the ocean and how the ocean brought them peace.

Miguel was a tall 6 feet 7 inch man from Mexico City.

He was dark skin (like that of the Natives Americans).

He was definitely taller than most Mexico City natives.

Miguel must have come from another region where native men grew as tall as he did.

He had a strong masculine figure (physically fit all around).

Miguel had long hair that ran just past his shoulder-blades (It was neatly placed back into a pony tail).

Miguel wore a very beautiful Italian-Suite: colored dark-burgundy.

His shoes were black leather (thin: like those of well-made Italian shoes).

Miguel's physical features did resemble that of a Native American: he bore high-cheek-bones (yet his face was long-thin oval shape: it was chiseled-out in a way that he looked like a Roman Soldier of the Americas!).

Americas!

Jana was mesmerized by him. His voice was deep (yet with softness)…

When Miguel had uttered his first words to Jana…the sounds were able to break her trance!

(When Jana was in deep thought she often committed to it completely…involuntarily unable to capture other sounds!)

Conscious at that very moment though: Jana could not believe her luck!

She thought, "Are my fortunes changing?"

Jana fell for Miguel immediately!

(She was not sure if Miguel felt the same way.)

(The indicators of his charm however leaned toward a "yes" *he does:)*)

In Miguel's mind he found Jana fascinating…it moved him to see her in deep-contemplation about something.

Jana was also physically beautiful to Miguel.

Miguel saw a fit-individual with soft-skin bearing beautiful hazel-grey eyes.

Miguel especially adored Jana's prominent cheeks that made her look like a Native American along with subtle distinct Anglo-Saxon features as well.

Miguel thought that maybe she spoke Spanish since she did have that look of Latin blood in her (They both did live in an environment densely-clustered with multiple strands of Spanish speaking peoples!).

So there sat the two humans: *sip**ping**-*their-drinks!

After talking for a while about the OCEAN and its currents, and how much they both liked it... and how it brought them **peace**: a *silence* **fell** over them.

$$s \, i \, l \, e \, n \, c \, e$$

s i l e n c e.

Somehow it did not seem awkward not to say *a word:* both felt at ease with one another.

It felt as though they had known each other *before*.

Jana felt happy in finding someone who she *instantaneously* felt at ease and fully attractive to her likings.

Miguel found it difficult to understand that he had become *speechless...* (and amazed in feeling this inner-**peace**-of-relaxation just-*being*-close-to-Jana!)

...Close to her.

...Close-to-her.

"Could this be the one?" Miguel thought.

Out of *all the times* he tried looking for *this precious*: he hadn't imaged that such a beauty would be *here*.....in a place he did not expect.

They both sat there *deeply* looking at each other: each *contemplating* the other in delight.

After more than *five* minutes had passed in *silent communication*: Miguel's phone interrupted their *deep-thoughts*.

Miguel reached into his phone and turned it *off.*

off!

off!!!

A bus finally roared by and vibrated the window where they sat....

...prompting Miguel to speak:

"would you like to walk by the ocean? It is…"

He was immediately interrupted:

"yes!" Jana enthusiastically responded!

Since each had their own car they decided to meet at the beach parking lot just south of Ocean Park Blvd. in Santa Monica.

Miguel walked her to her car and gave her *one more romantic glance.*

They both drove separately to the beach parking lot in-**EXHILARATION**-of-one-another.

They both ***FANTASIZED*** as to what would come *next...*

Next!...

Next!!!

At the beach parking lot near the boardwalk, Miguel had arrived first and was standing near his car and on the phone.

Five minutes later Jana pulled up and parked behind him.

He hung up the phone and headed toward her with a HUGE SMILE... Jana returned the smile with her own **enormous** expression!

She opened the door and stepped out and walked toward Miguel.

Without-the-slightest-thought-of-formality-or-etiquette she opened her arms and embraced him.

Miguel reached over and embraced her too.

Jana's head went up against his chest. Miguel smelled *SOOO* good!

Miguel lowered his head to hers and they both just stood there....thoughtless....in peace with one another.

After a *good* while of warming up to the idea Jana raised her head toward his. Miguel lowered himself and *they began* to *gently, softly,* and *slowly (ever-so-sweetly)* to kiss one another. KISS!!

KISS!!

KISS !!

Both were *immediately* aroused and tightened their grip on one another. Jana could feel his hardness pressed against her; and Miguel felt her soft breast pressed **hard** against him.

After a while they both guided each other toward *the water*.

When they reached the sand just past the board walk: Miguel sat down on the elevated concrete edge and removed his shoes and socks.

He then sat Jana down and carefully removed her shoes (feeling her *lower legs* and *feet* with his hand).

Miguel held each leg and feet for a while (as if giving them an exquisite massage before lowering one set and proceeding to the next).

Miguel asked her to wait while he placed the shoes in his car.

Jana stared at him as he moved with his naked feet to the car.

As he walked back: a growing excitement began to build up once more within Jana!

With every step that Miguel took: Jana began to feel her insides BURN with desire.

(Miguel noticed this immediately as he made his way to her... seeing Jana as she slowly and subtly swayed her torso in a small circular motion as if hypnotized.)

When the bodies met once more: Miguel gave Jana a gentle kiss on the forehead and then they both continued their journey to the water.

Could this be a dream?, Jana thought.

Could this really be happening?, they both thought.

When they reached the water both took in the salty view in front of them. It was about 5 in the afternoon.

Without-a-break-in-harmony they both headed North toward the Santa Monica Pier.

The sun was still strong: resisting the setting schedule in a couple of hours.

They walked and took in the cool breeze that came from the ocean.

Both walked about 500 yards past the pier (all the while holding hands and bumping into each other).

Then a pause entered their stride and they both sat together on the sand.

Jana asked him about his life and how he came to be here. Miguel told part of his story as Jana warmed up to him.

After a while Miguel said, "Hey, would you like to go in for a swim?"

Jana responded, "Well... it seems that the water is very cold. What with our clothes on!!!?"

"Let's **BARE-OFF** as much as we can legally do", Miguel responded. "There aren't many people and we are at a good distance from the pier and the crowd."

Miguel stood up amb-gràcia from the sand.

He took his coat, vest, tie, dress shirt, and trousers off and was left only wearing his designer underwear that wrapped smoothly around his groin and buttocks area.

Those underwear really looked like thin diving trunks, with the exception that they were made of pure cotton.

"Wow! What a beautiful muscular body!", Jana thought.

Jana extended her hands and Miguel helped her up.

They both stood there for a while.

She then took off her white skirt and green blouse.

Jana was left with a white, cotton bra and white cotton underwear that fit smoothly over her waist.

It looked like a two piece lingerie bathing suit!

...with beautiful vanilla crochet flowers at the ends.

Both felt good being together in front of the IMMENSITY-of-water that brought them peace.

After taking in the elements-that-abound and one another, Miguel ran toward the water.

He jumped in and began swimming inward toward the IMMENSITY about a hundred feet.

 Jana thought for a while...being hesitant because of the temperature of the water.

After several milliseconds, Jana *abandoned* her *doubting-thoughts* and ran towards Miguel.

Although the water was cold for Jana at first, she surprisingly felt *refreshed.* She hadn't felt like that in such a long time): Jana felt free: *free* to do the unusual and to do what was liberating... a moment in her life was realized that came completely *unexpected.*

Jana had never imagined that she would be with this beautiful man on *this* beautiful *day* today!

Beautiful

How did it come about? *Had* she done something special to deserve this luck of hers? *Had* she thought about it in the morning when she woke up *completely alone* in her bed (with the exception of her cat!)?

It truly was a blessing!

This rendezvous with an *unknown future* made her feel like a child...not knowing what would happen next!

As Jana swam toward Miguel she felt the breath-of-life *enter her*! She was *not alone*! *Not alone*!.....at least not at that moment.....*not alone* in such a long while.

laysat wahdaha

ليسي تحودها

No make-up, no clothes of fashion: just her and her underwear!

"Wow! Hoouray!"

...were the onomatopoeia-expressions of inspirations within Jana at *that* moment!

"This feels so cold! But I feel **sO**

energized!"

"energized to survive! ...no, no...correction...energized to *live life*!"

live life!

Jana spoke these proclamations in her mind as she breast-stroked her way towards Miguel.

As Jana neared Miguel...He told her: "Come, let's get a little closer inland to catch a wave!"

Miguel then pointed and said...

"I see some waves forming from afar."

Miguel and Jana moved a little inland and after a while a wave came. Miguel quickly instructed her to swim toward shore as the wave neared.

She swam and swam and suddenly Jana felt the wave thrust her forward.

At that moment Jana was completely involved with the motion of the wave.

Jana felt as if she were *a dolphin*...in unison...as *one with the ocean*!

The *thrust* exhilarated her to the point that she SCREAMED!

As the motion continued, Jana began curving her body in rhythm with the wave!

Her body's movements resembled that of a tadpole...

...but instead of side to side beginning with the tail, Jana motioned her body up and down, beginning with her head!

[a NEW SPECIES in the ocean! Oh my J!!!:)]

As the wave dissipated into white fizzles, Jana noticed that Miguel was still waiting for his own wave.

When it came, Miguel took it! As he neared Jana toward the end of the force of the wave, Miguel jumped off it and swam towards her.

When they finally reached each other, they embraced—again she felt his hardness develop.

They stood there together as the small waves crashed against them.

All of a sudden, Jana could feel his penis without the cotton cloth!

—It had ESCAP*ED!*

It wanted Jana and she wanted it!

As they began walking out of the water, Miguel immediately noticed the escap**ee** and squatted down to hide the fugitive!

Jana joined him in the squatting position.

Both knelt down on the sand, taking a leap of trust in matrimony, pleasantly receiving the cool-white-foaming-water:

The sacred foam was at about Jana's shoulders.

Both resumed their embrace.

The rush-of-water encouraged them even more to sustain the sacred plunge! Both began to kiss each other *uncontrollably.*

uncon t r oll ab l y!

YUM!

Both beings embraced eachother with such a passion that Jana wasn't sure if they were going to do it right then and there.....on a public beach!

The idea of *doing it on a public beach* excited Jana even more!

Jana reached down and grabbed his *p r e c i o u s.*

Jana was surprised at the large size of Miguel's penis....a very thick diameter with a long reach!

Jana began to stroke it under the white-CURTAIN-of-Sacred-Water.

With their continued kissing and Jana stroking of his precious, Miguel become very aroused.

At that moment Miguel felt like tearing Jana's remaining clothes and DEVOURING her!

Miguel took a deep breath through his nostrils (since his lips were occupied).

He tried very hard to calm himself down.

...he was beginning to climax!

climaX!

climax!

Miguel breathed (and breathed deeply).

...this allowed him to temporarily sustain the *ripping climax*!

Miguel then began *a rhythm* of breathing **slowly** with his eyes closed...allowing him TIME to reach beneath THE-WHITE-CURTAIN toward Jana's va-gī-na.

Miguel **gently**-slipped-his-fingers into her panties and began stroking Jana's cli**TO R**is*!*

Jana became extremely aroused and kissed him even more passionately.

Miguel's regional and precise massages intensified as he sensed *that* was electrifying Jana!

For every five strokes to her clitoris, Miguel inserted his index and middle finger into her vagina.

Jana m**oa**ned and m**oa**ned and m**oa**ned*!!!*

Miguel had learned this stroke technique from what his previous lovers had requested of him during the initiation stage of *play*!

Miguel too began to moan as their hands swiftly moved *under the water*.

The pleasure was **so intense** that each rested their respective head against the neck of the other.

LEV erage was at play!

As the strokes increased in speed both **moaned-and-moaned** until both were about to come at the *same time!*

As Miguel heard her coming in a big **MOAN**, he let loose his pleasure-of-ecstasy in a stream-of-semen that, **he felt**, could *cover the world!*

exhausted   exhausted

exhausted after *climaxing*, both held each other gently as the calming white streams of waves became smaller and continued to brush against them.

exhausted

Both beings looked at each other and gave each other *one last kiss* before standing.

As they stood, both maneuvered their respective under-wears into place.

Both beings then began their magical *waltz* back to the dry shore.

Their strides out of water felt **majestic**.

Each being felt At ease with the other.

...eliminating any need for verbal communication.

Allowing both beings to take in their surroundings to the **fullest** without-words.

[a majestic landscape...a *hidden place* usually blurred by the filter of their encasements...but not in this case!!!]

The SOL was almost gone from sight...preparing a path to begin *a new day in other lands*!

As they left the Waters Miguel spoke:

"Listen, you see that red-tiled home over there?"

Jana looked up to the pointed direction.

"It is my home. Come with me and we'll wash up and rest. Is that okay?"

Jana was caught by surprise.

She didn't know what to make of it at that instant.

After a good *511 jiffies* (in Fermi counts) of contemplation, Jana smiled at Miguel and nodded "Yes"!

Jana could not believe what was happening.

She felt so happy... **SO VERY VERY** *happy!!!*

Jana did not want to think further of the unfolding possibilities...she didn't want to *jink*s the wonderful rhythm of **the song!**

the song!

Jana wanted to live *the moment* for what *the moment* was and not what *the moment* was to become or could become.

Jana could not ask for anything more at this time:

She was completely content.

PART **2** of 7
A BUSINESS MAN FROM MEXICO

Chapter 9

A Brief Look at Miguel's Earlier Life in Mexico

Miguel made his home base in the beach city of Santa Monica, California (in the County of Los Angeles). As a Mexican business man who sells Mexican exported artistry goods and packaged baked goods and other developing products, Miguel enjoys the art of sharing his discoveries to the world!

His strong love for his Mexican culture in general, and for the various cultures that exist within Mexico, have a solid foundation in his mind and how he lives his life.

Miguel shared with Jana that since he was a child he loved to see the artisans in the street selling their original works of art: everything from beautiful woven rugs to carved figures.

Miguel was fascinated by their skill and their imagination.

As a consequence of such influences, Miguel attempted at an early age to do some sort of artwork himself.

Yet the inspiration did not translate to magnificent works of art: he did not quite have the knack for it.

Through the process of trial and error, Miguel soon learned that his knack was not making works of art but selling them!

In many ways he took this gift of selling as an art form in itself...to attract buyers to his merchandise in creative ways that other sellers had not attempted.

At sixteen years of age, Miguel made his first `major` milestone growth in sells when he had decided to sell baked goods made by his neighbor named Martha.

Martha was an old woman of eighty-one who was very good at making original pastries.

Martha had never really sold anything herself. All her baked products were made for her large family. No one in the family ever took an interest in doing business selling baked goods: and so her recipes remained hidden.

Martha had been married since she was a young teenager, and her main occupation in life was to care for her eight children who now looked after her at her old age.

All her children had become educators for one reason or another.

Martha became a widow at the age of fifty two and never remarried. Miguel met her 25 years after the death of her husband who died of heart-failure.

After 4 years of knowing Martha, it then dawned on Miguel to make a business proposition to Martha about selling her goods at his mobile shack stand he had built himself.

Miguel sold in the streets artisan goods and now included baked goods with Martha's help.

Many of his best-selling artisan goods consisted of party favorites.

These party favorite orders gave Miguel large quantities of revenue in a short period of time which allowed him to make his businesses grow quickly.

Miguel knew instinctively which products would sell and so he focused on certain artisan products that were used in birthday parties, weddings, and other special social events.

For orders that were placed in advance, the customer chose from booklets; booklets created by Miguel showing pictures of his products and their specifications and discounts if the customer decided to order large quantities.

Everyone trusted Miguel because for him "the customer" was top priority. He went out of his way to please customers who approached his stand, and made sure that orders placed in advance were fulfilled at the time requested and delivered securely.

Miguel had made business arrangements not only with artisans but also with local drivers and packaging companies.

These middle-partners would receive a bonus if they delivered on time or earlier. The partners loved Miguel because he brought in unexpected and needed business for them.

Miguel had proven to them that his word was solid....they received immediate payment with bonus!

As to the baked goods, Martha was hesitant at first since she had never made any business arrangements in her life!

Martha's offspring knew Miguel and trusted him completely...which made it easy for Martha to say yes!

As the baking goods business project started, one of the ways Miguel made her feel comfortable was hire reliable and respectful people to help her with the preparations of the baked goods. These hired hands were mainly Christians.

Miguel did surprisingly well with the baked goods and gave Martha thirty-four percent of the profit of sales made after costs. The remaining net profit of the baked goods was divided between Miguel personally and his separate-entity corporate baking business (which he wholly controlled and owned).

Miguel took charge of getting all the ingredients delivered to Martha and her crew.

Miguel also safeguarded the recipes by having each crew member only do certain aspects of the baked-goods preparations.

Some would come in and prepare part of the dough at one hour and then another crew would complete it.

Miguel made sure they never crossed each other or knew each other.

The baking required, among many considerations, special density specifications, bake times, and ingenious additive ingredients to make the finished baked products irresistible to any taste buds!

Miguel also had a special crew that did the actual baking and another crew for the after-baking decorative add-ons!

At the end, there was a 7th step for 16 of the 61 baked products. For those products Miguel had a young boy his age prepare and add the specialty made syrup....which required considerable skill and know-how. J

As orders consistently grew from outside local convenient stores and later supermarkets, Miguel was able to purchase his first 7-acre space which housed his baking hangers at the outskirts of Mexico City.

Martha later became the executive supervisor of the processing of her sixteen big selling baked goods in addition to the moderate selling ones that were slowly but surely gaining popularity-traction.

After about 3 years of doing successful business growth in Miguel's baking division, Martha fell ill.

Doctors could not explain it except that it was old age kicking in. Consequently, although her health became temporarily stable, she was not able to continue performing as she once had.

Martha decided to call Miguel to her house for a meeting.

Miguel came quietly into her bedroom.

She had been sleeping for quite some time. In fact, Martha began spending most of her time sleeping!

She was taking lots of pain killers to keep the pain in her bones at a minimal.

"Ven, siéntate aquí" She told Miguel in Spanish. [1*] *[English translation of Spanish text of Martha at end of this chapter]*

He sat down at a chair next to her. "Hola Marta, ¿cómo sigues?" He asked her how she felt.

[2*] "Igual", she responded. [3*]"Quiero que sepas que te estimo mucho. Quiero que sigas por el camino que has escogido; tienes talento en los asuntos de negocios."

Martha went on to tell Miguel that he should go north to the United States of America, to California in particular, to grow his business in that country as well.

Martha also told Miguel about dreams she had of him meeting a young woman in need of help:

"This woman is your destiny!" she told him in Spanish.

"¿Es algo positivo o negativo esta mujer de mi destino?", preguntó Miguel. ["Is it something positive or negative this woman of my destiny?" he asked.

[4*] "La vida querido niño siempre esta lleno de lo positive y los negativos; no mires la vida en esa forma. Tu destino será lo que será sin tomar en cuenta el positive o los negativos."

"Eres una persona alegre con una gran personalidad. A todos les caes muy bien. Le sacas lo bueno de cada persona."

"¡Tu carisma es tu don!"

"Toma. Esta carpeta contiene todas las recetas que han vendido muy bien. Aquí también hay algunas que estaba formulando y no te las había enseñado".

"Abre un negocio de panes en los Estados Unidos. Y, también abre otros tipos de negocios allí. ¡Te ira bien, lo sé!"

"Gracias Maite" Miguel said affectionately. He took the notebook, bent over and kissed Martha on the forehead, and left.

Miguel was eighteen when he left Mexico City.

Like all good Mexicans with ambitions to the North (unconscious of the planned-designed-exploitations formulated between adjacent governments in secret to push workers pass the border to provide cheap wages to mischievous employers), Miguel packed his bags and went to the northern Mexican border.

However, unlike many **un**fortunate Mexicans in Mexico, Miguel was financially well off in his country and because of that: he was able to cross legally north of the Mexican/American border.

In fact, Miguel had gained considerable wealth selling his varied goods, all of which started off at his self-built little mobile shack he had worked from for a year.

After that year, he began selling his goods to local convenient stores and then supermarkets. From there, he packaged his goods and sold them across Mexico, including Chiapas.

Slowly his goods made their way across Central America...as far as Costa Rica...climbing slowly into the Panama Markets and edging closer to South America!

Miguel became a success story!

His brand of artisan goods called "Magolie" sold well. His pastry division called "Marchita" made even more revenue!

Marchita baked goods were synonymous with excellence and uniqueness. Miguel took it to heart to use excellent and whole-foods ingredients, not short changing the customers. He was very cognizant in many ways including in what went into the products he manufactured and sold.

Many mass-producing pastry companies did not do likewise...using instead artificial ingredients and unhealthy oils that caused them illness in the long run. And now, the the use of genetically modified ingredients poses even a greater danger to the masses.

Miguel's businesses in Mexico were expanding quite rapidly but prudently...creating strong foundations that would last beyond the millenniums!

It is as though Miguel was born to know business! ...as if the successful knowledge of business transactions were in his genes!

Genes!

…embedded programming not taught! Given.

...Like that of the spider who already has the programming in its being to build spider-webs without ever being taught: Given.)

As to the baked goods division, Martha would take her profit share and give most of it to her sons who loved her and cared for her.

Her offspring too had grown considerably wealthy due to Miguel's innovative selling techniques.

Notwithstanding, success in Miguel's baked goods business would not have been big if it hadn't been for Martha's recipes.

Looking further back in Miguel's past, he was orphaned and had no family he knew of. He was abandoned at an early age of about two months by his mother whom he could not remember.

He was left in front of the steps of St. Augustus Catholic Church.

Some parishioners found him on the steps, covered in blankets, lying in an opened wooden bread basket!

From that point of his existence, Miguel became part of the Catholic Church. The parish priest assigned a group of local nuns to care for him instead of leaving him for chance to the Mexican orphanage.

Miguel grew up in a convent of nuns who loved him as their own.

Since these nuns ran a primary and secondary boarding school that went up to high school, Miguel was able to stay with them until he decided to venture out trying to make a living which began when he constructed his selling cart!

Chapter Notes:

English Translation of Spanish Text:

Text Translation of Martha's dialogue referenced by a number and an Asterisk:

1 "Come,Sit down here"*

2 "The Same"*

3 "I want you to know that I hold you in high regard. I love you, you are a good boy with a good heart" "I want you to continue the course you have chosen; you have talent in the realm of business."*

4   Life, my dear boy is always filled with the positive and the negatives, don't look at life in that way. Your destiny will be what it will be, regardless of positive or negatives. You are a happy person with a great personality. Everyone has a great liking to you. You bring out the best in people; your charisma is your gift!"*

5 "Here" she continued. "Take this notebook, it contains all my recipes for the goods that have sold so well. Open a bakery business in the United States, and open other types of businesses. You will do well. I know it!"*

Chapter Ten
Miguel Explores California

When Miguel arrived at the border between San Ysidro and Tijuana, he decided to travel by car along the coast of California. He wanted to explore and get a firsthand account of the state of California of which Martha had told him lie his destiny!

Miguel's businesses still operated in Mexico, but he wanted to expand it to a place that would possibly be his second home: Southern California.

Currently, Miguel owned two houses: one in Mexico City and the other in the outskirts of Districto Federal.

Miguel also owned several facilities for the production of his products. He left his top managers in charge and got daily reports on the progress of different aspects of his businesses.

So, in the summer of 1988, Miguel took some clothing and headed toward his destiny. He was a young man on a mission of exploration and realization.

As Miguel drove, he took in the breathtaking views of the Pacific Ocean. On his journey, he stayed in modest inns. His rental car was a 1988 Lexus.

In Mexico City, Miguel had met some clients who lived in Malibu California. They had offered him a guest house on their property to stay for as long as he wanted.

He accepted!

However, before making a complete stop there, Miguel drove on to San Francisco to see the city of many beautiful faces: both architecturally and in human forms.

San Francisco was definitely something he had not expected. In contrast to other cities along the coast, San Francisco's tall streets where littered with busy people moving about with such determination: Everyone seemed to be going and coming non-stop.

As Miguel explored the San Francisco streets, he came upon Castro Street. He put coins in the meter and headed to a quaint café that sold sandwiches. It had arches decorating the perimeter

of its establishment. The arches had huge colorful
flowers at each corner of the squared perimeter.

Miguel thought: "Wow! ¡Que mezcla de color y
arquitectura!" He loved it! It was very charming.
The color of the flowers where red, orange, yellow,
green, blue, purple. The paint of the overall
building was a beautiful pastel of adobe.

But the surprise was inside!

As Miguel stepped in he noticed immediately the
long corridor that ran to the end of the building. It
was set up as a bar; but it had nice, small, wooden
mahogany tables. They were square shaped with
the edges made round in an elaborate artistic
semicircle.

The cafe was completely full of people, mostly
men. The man at the counter greeted him with a
smile as did the men who stared at him from their
tables.

Miguel was escorted to a table and sat down on a
wooden chair. Immediately a man who was in the
back end of the bar table came over with a menu
and greeted him.

"Good afternoon sir! I have Hope and Faith and so I'm encouraged that you're having a pleasant day!"

"Yes, thank you", Miguel responded with an accent.

"Here's the menu. Take your time to look at it and I'll be back soon."

The man was dressed in tight black leather shorts that ended high above his knees. He wore a black t-shirt with the symbol of the café:

That symbol was the colorful flowers that decorated the ends of the outside of the establishment.

The café was called...

"Flowers of Love".

The menu had an array of choices. For the meat eaters, there were all types of sandwiches from meatloaf to roast beef to a variety of fish with a choice of 25 cheeses!

There were also 10 different breads to choose from!: Cuban bread, Ciabatta, fruit bread, multigrain, oat, pumpernickel, rye, sourdough, wheat, and white.

The customer could add to their sandwich tomato, romaine lettuce, sliced carrots, white or red onion, or just have it plain with meat only or just adding to it cheese or humus, or a combination!

For the vegetarian, they had the same, but substituted the meat with a choice of tofu, guacamole or extra romaine or spinach greens.

For the vegan, it offered the same but without cheese (which was substituted with a special blend of 7 choices of humus which tasted like cheese but was not!). [oh my J! How inventive!:]

All three types used separate cooking utensils, frying pans or grill, and accessories for the preparation of the food.

Desserts included home-made pie slices of peach, lemon meringue, and pumpkin pie. It also included double fudge cake or chocolate chip cake.

[yum...i definitely need that right now!]

As to the drinks: soda, beer, fresh squeeze citrus juices and a good selection of Mexican juice drinks called "aguas frescas" (Durazno, Guayaba, Horchata, Jamaica, Papaya, Sandia, y Tamarindo:).

Miguel felt like he was in an eatery in Mexico City! All the food was prepared fresh daily with local vendors bringing in the raw ingredients in the morning.

The atmosphere was pleasant and the food smelled delicious! These guys really cared about their product: Miguel sensed it immediately.

After he ordered, Miguel began to look around.

He immediately noticed how men were sitting too close to each other. And then he noticed some of them holding hands or looking passionately at eachother.

He immediately understood that he was in a gay establishment.

No new thing for Miguel: plenty of gay people in Mexico City. It was now widely accepted to be who you are {in all aspects}.

Miguel felt right at home.

San Francisco was like Mexico City in many ways:
a unique arena where the colors of all the
imagination found their home! There were artists
of all types, each one had its own appetite!

On the topic of sexuality, Miguel was strictly a
woman kind of a guy. In fact, he *adored* the
breast-of-women. Their bosom provided for him a
maternal as well as a sexual arousal that he needed;
as most men need...at least in regards to sexuality.

Yet Miguel refrained from any sexual encounter
with women up to the present. For now, his mind
was solely occupied in his businesses and the
growth of them.

Chapter Eleven
Beatrice

Miguel's first sexual encounter occurred ten years later in 1998. He had since established himself as a major importer of Mexican goods in the United States of America: including the commercial distribution of his successful Marchita brand pastries in American stores.

It was after this economic footing in the American business world that Miguel finally accepted a sexual advance by a woman who worked for him:

Beatrice

 Beatrice was his personal secretary who would communicate to him all incoming calls and would type up all contracts with vendors and bankers.

(Miguel required a written agreement with every business entity he dealt with since in the past he had experienced being taken to court and not having a physical written agreement to prove a business understanding with two bankers on a loan regarding shared venture revenues he had gotten involved in.)

(Although he won the verdict {worth 7 million dollars in interest savings and commissioned royalties}, Miguel found it necessary from that point forward to confirm every business agreement to be executed in writing...not allowing any further business proceedings to evolve until it was signed and notarized by both respective representative attorneys to the venture.)

(As to this legal dilemma he had had with these bankers...Miguel was saved by the jury since he provided them with numerous transactions that had been done in the past demonstrating their mutual regular business dealings he had with these banker partners that proved his point. Miguel also had receipts and phone messages left on his business numbers in California supporting further his claims. Miguel had been spared a *crooked deal*!)

Now to the present change in Miguel's life:

Beatrice!

Beatrice was a lovely beauty from Vera Cruz, Mexico. She had German and Spanish mix in her blood and her beautiful long straight light brown hair gave her a "Barbie" type face...adding a European touch of beauty.

When Miguel had interviewed her for the vacant position, Beatrice had an impressive resume working as a secretary for 9 years at Avioneta-Mexicana Airlines.

As to Miguel's analysis of this gorgeous woman on a personal level, he did not, although she was beautiful from the outside, see that her beauty extended much inwardly as to her personality---at least not to the likings of Miguel.

Beatrice was very domineering; she wanted things in her control at all times. She was not a workaholic, but she did see it necessary to be in control of everything she did. Beatrice was quite outspoken and did speak what was on her mind.

At first glance, one would assume she was a timid beauty.

However, after a few enunciations coming from her mouth, it was apparent that Beatrice was something else...a person seeking to take control...to take charge!

A woman in a man's world...and she was looking at changing *that* landscape arrangement!

Beatrice had her own side-business selling nutritional products for the healthy minded person. She was in tip-top shape with beautiful breasts of about a "C" size cup and beautiful buttocks that protruded from her slim 27 year old waist.

Beatrice's skin tone was fair in complexion: the color and scent of her being was *fresh vanilla*!

Beatrice always wore Christian Dior's *J'Adore* and always smelled magnificent!

(Miguel was not a fan of woman wearing perfumes, but this fragrance was *his* exception!)

Beatrice would always go to the gym before she reported to work at 10 a.m. She would somehow manage to work out, bathe, eat, and beautify herself before she came in each morning!

Wow!!!

The sexual encounter Miguel experienced from Beatrice came unexpected. It all began one early evening at the office. To be exact, it was July 4th 1998.

Miguel was finishing up some agreements over the phone with some of his clients when Beatrice, who was single at the time, came into the office looking rather happy from her usual serious and demanding personality:d

 "¡Hola Miguel! Mira, ¿que te parece si vamos juntos a ver el desfile de fuego en la playa de Redondo Beach?"

"Tengo algunos amigos allí que van a tener una merendá y me han invitado a compartir tiempo con ellos."

Beatrice was inviting Miguel to view fireworks at Redondo Beach beach, just south of the pier. She had been invited by some friends.

Beatrice knew, after working for Miguel for nearly five years, that he had no significant other. Miguel spent most of his time conducting his businesses: regularly having dinner with clients in order to finalize business deals.

Early on Miguel had decided to hold off from the drama of a relationship since he knew that relationships required time; personal time he felt he couldn't commit-to in a relationship at this stage in his career.

Miguel had seen arguments by couples when he was at St. Augustus Catholic Church in Mexico City...bringing their unresolved issues to the parish priests.

While serving at the parish office as an office assistant part-time, Miguel could hear the diverse arguments that couples had---all ranging from money matters, infidelity, the demanding of one partner for more time of the other partner to spend in the relationship, to outright physical and verbal violence coming from one or both parties!

Miguel had learned that the financial or cultural background differences of couples did not matter: the issues seemed to be the same across the spectrum.

The issues presented to the priests, as Miguel heard the conversations going on in the next room from the vantage point of the parish reception area involved matters of complexity in selfishness or a lack of understanding or a lack of collaboration; such matters which Miguel strongly felt to be counterproductive to his goals.

As such, Miguel, although he did encounter some *beautiful* women in his early life, decided to refrain from his inner desires to want to physically *devour* them!

d e v o u r them!

Miguel would in his mind intentionally paint faces on the beautiful women that came his way as being undesirable to him: creating faces of fat pigs, possums, or ugly business men who ate at a faster rate than their metabolisms could burn off!

This *mind programming* worked for *the most part*.

However, this tactic was becoming less and less effective as time passed!

So a time came when this avoidance-technique could no longer work; at least not with Beatrice; he would see her every day!

E VER Y DA Y!

It was extremely hard to keep that negative, false imaginary painted face on Beatrice's head when everything physically about her *spelled* DESIRE!

D E S I R E !

And so the *Spell of Desire* took its course; the hormones in Miguel's body were taking over Miguel's logic on the night of the light show!

Miguel could not *resist* her advances as they sat in darkness with other couples watching the fireworks on the beach (south of the Redondo Beach Pier).

Miguel felt the hand of Beatrice embrace his hip. The tug was firm; extremely firm for someone who seemed so petit!

Beatrice then casually pressed herself against him and leaned her head on his shoulder.

Miguel's hormonal senses flared up like never before!

Miguel felt his penis getting hard and harder...the warmth of her body was caressing a human being that was slowly and quickly letting go!

The word "resistance" no longer had its force on Miguel that **fireworks** night!

Beatrice then slid her left hand toward his penis; she immediately became *aroused* when she felt his massive penis as hard as **STONE!**

Beatrice stroked it gently with her hand and then hard at intervals of about three soft strokes to one hard stroke.

 Miguel sat there not knowing whether to put an end to it or let it continue. While he thought, he allowed it to continue. Miguel did not turn to her, although the desire was extremely strong to touch Beatrice and kiss her madly.

Miguel just stood there feeling the pleasure building with every *hard* stroke that came his way!

He began to quietly moan; Beatrice could hear him and was strongly aroused by his moans! (Although she could not see Miguel in the darkness, Beatrice began to *climax* to his sounds!).

As Miguel began to climax, he clasped the slippery sand beneath the blanket. Beatrice's strokes went *on*; but this time they were *faster* and all *hard* strokes. Miguel could not conceal it anymore and began to moan *louder*: trying to keep it inaudible (but to no avail).

After several deep audible moans, he moaned one big *quiet* moan...letting out the *juices of life* from his penis.

As Miguel's moans subsided, Beatrice knew he had come. She then began to stroke it *ever so* gently. Beatrice felt the wetness of his pants and knew he had come... and come *big*!

Miguel sat their exhausted by the tremendous effort he expelled.

Beatrice spoke. "Vámonos a mi apartamento; te limpiaré bien para que puedas descansar."

Miguel knew that her invitation to go to her Redondo Beach apartment was her desire to have him for *the night.*

Beatrice wanted to hold on to *a man* who had in the past consistently shunned her advances.

Beatrice wanted to *hold him* as if she *owned him*...even if just for the night!

It was Saturday night and Miguel had made it a routine never to conduct heavy business on Sunday—he was an observant Catholic (to a certain extent).

And, although he hardly went to Church, he made it a habit to relax most of that day.

Miguel accepted.

They stood up and Beatrice wrapped the blanket around her and Miguel. She said good bye to her friends, who were seated about seven feet ahead. They knew Beatrice had *conquered her prize* for the night and that she would be well.

Beatrice drove a convertible Audi **600**.

As they drove to her apartment, Miguel was having second thoughts; thinking hard if he wanted this to continue. This *eruption* of a night had gone against his discipline to stay focused on his career.

He was at a road's end!

Miguel now wanted freedom from his self-imposed confines. It had been ten years since his arrival to the United States and his businesses had flourished.

Miguel was at this point convinced that it was time to be free socially and to explore. Beatrice's desires became the point of no return for him.

When they entered her apartment, which was located on Manhattan Beach Blvd., just east of Aviation Blvd, on the second floor, unit **9B**, Beatrice *quietly* led Miguel to her bathroom.

She undressed him and then herself. Then Beatrice led Miguel into the ample shower area. *Quite exquisitely* Beatrice looked as she turned on the running water.

As the water poured, Beatrice used her hands to wash Miguel's body: she noticed immediately that his penis had grown.

Again!

Miguel had a wonderful thick penis about eight inches long with a girth of about 5.2 inches.

Beatrice immediately knelt in the shower area which was large enough to make both of them fit in comfortably.

As Beatrice lowered herself, she opened her mouth and clasped it around Miguel's penis.

Miguel could do no more than to begin to moan again.

Beatrice was magnificent at sexually pleasing any man! Her large brown breast and her well-trimmed groin area were well figured and ready for duty!

Miguel held her hair as Beatrice continued to **indulge** in his manhood.

He stood there speechless and continued to moan.

Beatrice's head movements continued, but now they became faster and with more pressure.

Miguel had not come in so long that he had plenty of juices; and since he was not conditioned to this type of excitement, he could not control himself:

Miguel burst into a loud groan (like that of a **fierce tiger**) and came inside Beatrice's mouth.

Beatrice swallowed his semen.

...slowly.

Miguel had meant so much to her; he had provided a good paying job for her when her luck had gone sour (with a load of credit card bills becoming over due at a fast rate).

Miguel had saved her from financial ruin.

¡Me salvó!

Beatrice had always found Miguel to be a *very attractive man* but had not made a strong enough move on him until she had decided that enough was enough.

Beatrice too had *held herself* in the past from a definitive attack on her desires to have him.

She didn't want to spoil a good working relationship.

Beatrice did make moderate advances on Miguel, but always left the harmony open for him to complete.

Miguel never completed those harmonies when Beatrice started them (she was left wanting him even more!).

Two Desire Forces denying their physical attraction! Tension was building quietly and loudly behind the scenes! A burst was inevitable at some point as these two beings saw eachother almost every day, year after year.

Burst was definitely on cue and it was beginning to transform itself into a ticking time bomb whose indefinite designated time was becoming more and more definitive!

Miguel's acceptance to the fireworks show was his *completion of the harmony*: and so Beatrice made her move.

Beatrice desperately wanted Miguel; and now this man was in her apartment!

¡En mi apartamento!

In my apartment!!!...

... Beatrice **roused** herself quietly into

euphOria.

She stood up and seductively kissed Miguel on his neck.

Miguel helped her bathe but had not gone to her groin.

...he was still doubting his actions.

Miguel did, however, begin to unconsciously kiss her nipples, and then he *held her* near him.

After they had rinsed and dried each other thoroughly, intermingled with kisses and tight hugs, Beatrice led Miguel to her huge window at the corner of the large bathroom.

They both saw each other in the image reflected by the light and the glass.

Beatrice was happy, and Miguel began to get thrilled beyond control!

After more embraces and kisses intensely amplified by the images each saw in the mirror, Beatrice led Miguel to her bed.

She knew he was ready!

They stood *in darkness* together.

It was as if the entire Universe descended upon them...ready to take a moment into the hand of Creation.

The only light coming in was that of the street light outside. The temperature was very warm—Beatrice's thermostat was set to 24 degrees Celsius. He body temperature was even hotter!!!

Miguel was *dry*, so to speak, since he had *come* twice!

This is exactly what Beatrice wanted (and had planned...an experienced sex-maiden!).

Beatrice knew Miguel had no one, and she knew that he would come quickly if it was his first orgasm in a while.

So Beatrice had *prepared him* for bed!

She wanted him *to last* so that she could enjoy him and climax with him *still inside*.

Beatrice was a curious creature!

She could come at the simple thought of any type of high-sexual-arousement.

Beatrice had already *come* twice that night just being a tool of pleasure for Miguel.

MIGUEL!

The thought of *doing it* with *Miguel* just threw-

her-**Over**boa_rd!

l-i-t-e-r-a-l-l-y!

Miguel pulled Beatrice close again: felling every
bit of her contours: her breasts were soft but
F I R M (and they were warm to him).

warm **Hot!**

He could feel Beatrice's nipples hard on his chest
wanting to drill him if they could!

The feel of those solid nard torpedoes thrilled
Miguel way too much!!!

His arousal became unbearable...to this man who
had self-imposed celibacy for more than 20 years!

20 years!

(¡que pendejo! pues clarines pendecito
¡pendisoso!)

Miguel then slightly pressed his body a bit harder towards Beatrice...she felt for the first time that night his manhood pressed against her groin.

Beatrice opened her legs about 4 inches apart, raised herself up (using Miguel as an anchor).

She then grabbed his penis and slowly and rhythmically lowered her vagina onto his manhood!

Miguel felt her *wetness*.

Instinctly, he gently stroked her upper labia with his hardness...feeling her wet hairs brush up against him.

Miguel lowered his head slightly and kissed Beatrice.

Oh she took him in.

"Could this really be happening?" she asked herself in her mind.

"I can't believe it!"

"So long I've waited for this very moment".

Instinctly too Beatrice responded by opening her mouth wider. Miguel thrust his tongue into her mouth.

The tongues danced together in delight!

Beatrice clasped Miguel's hair with her right hand and his neck with her left hand: massaging it gently in ecstasy.

They stood there in rhythmic motion for at least ten minutes without any penetration!

No Penetration!

{How could anyone resist!?}

After the dance of tongues, Beatrice lowered her feet to the ground and walked onto her bed.

Miguel followed her with his **MASSIVE ERECTION** displayed!

That **HUGE MUSCLE** sought relief!

Beatrice pushed herself up to the upper part of the bed and lay on her back belly up!

Miguel immediately moved up on top of her; he did not completely lay on her for fear of hurting her.

Oh...but he wanted to HU*RT HER!*

He wanted to **POUN**CE on her with-all-his-**MIGHT**...a w*ill* controlled by his hormones... irrationally driven by ecstasy!

Beatrice grabbed Miguel's penis *gently,* and *skillfully* led it into her vagina.

Miguel loved the softness of Beatrice.

He was about to thrust himself into her when he thought (in his gentleman-like-responsible-way-of-thinking [bullshit!]) to tell her that this display of sexuality did not mean that he wanted a serious relationship with her.

Miguel wanted to have her physically but he did not want a relationship with her. He had deduced their compatibility to be not-so-compatible.

In his mind Miguel knew that their personalities would not mix well for a long-term relationship.

A party pooper disclaimer for sure.

Miguel `stopped` himself, lifted his head, and told her:

"Bella-trice, quiero que sepas que eres muy hermosa, pero si continuamos, no quiere decir que vamos *a ser* una pareja; te deseo mucho, pero ahora no estoy listo para una relación seria."

Beatrice gently touched his head with her fingers and said:

"Miguel, ya sé que quizá no seamos pareja; pero te deseo físicamente y quiero tenerte **¡dentro de mi!** aun si es lo única forma de tenerte."

"Entiendo y estoy de acuerdo contigo Miguel:"

"¡Por favor dame tu pene dame tu ser!"

"¡DAME!"

With that said, Miguel thrust himself inside Beatrice; held his penis in her, *deeply* penetrating her.

Beatrice yelled *loudly* in ecstasy, grabbed his outer thighs and pulled then hard against herself.

Her intense hands prompted Miguel to begin a `rough`-rhythmic (or `Robotic`)-penetration of "in and out"!

IN and **OUT**

After every five insertions into Beatrice's vagina, Miguel would *thrust himself* hard against her and momentarily hold it in.

Beatrice moaned louder with every hard thrust that was accompanied by a pause: she was in *pure* bliss and just could not control her thoughts.

Beatrice kept her eyes closed most of the time: *taking in* the "feelings and thoughts" that she perceived rushed inside his mind.

She would only open them to reinforce Miguel's elegant body thrusting himself into her!

What a sight!

Beatrice came once, twice, three times and then again after 12 minutes of *pure* ecstasy.

At this point, Miguel began to moan and was unable to hold his breathing; his body began to palpitate faster and faster; his hips moved at such a fast speed that Beatrice could hardly hold onto him with her hands.

Miguel raised her legs and spread them further apart...thrusting his penis deeper and deeper into her VAGINA!

The point of climax was arriving: he gave a *loud* rhythmically palpitating fast moan (with as much as 16 beats PER measure), as if someone was hurting him.

...and then he

...delivered his manhood juices to Beatrice: expelling the seeds of Creation!

Beatrice was able to come one-last-time *right before* Miguel came!

Miguel crouched up above Beatrice, pulling his penis from her after expelling, what he felt, was the last of his semen. (He felt a testicular pull-pain).

Miguel carefully knelt and lowered his head near her legs, as if in a child's pose, and breathed deeply: silently regaining his breath.

Beatrice skillfully raised her upper torso and gently touched his head with her hands and kissed it.

Beatrice then slightly rested her head on top of Miguel's (still embracing it).

They were both drenched in sweat: from their heads *all the way down* to their toes!

After 34 inhalations, Miguel moved to one side of the bed, postured himself to his side and slept; Beatrice turned and held him...situated behind him.

After a while Beatrice wrapped the large white bed sheet around *her and Miguel,* and then she pressed against him **even** more...she too *fell* into sleep.

They slept and slept and slept in the warmth of the room and their sweat kept them warm as it slowly evaporated from their bodies.

What a night to remember!

Early the next morning, Miguel awoke.

Beatrice lay asleep.

Miguel carefully and gently kissed her on the forehead and got out of bed.

Miguel showered again, this time by himself.

After cleansing, Miguel noticed that his slacks were stained with large amounts of dried semen! So he decided to keep his shirt untucked.

Miguel left Beatrice a note giving his thanks for a beautiful night!

Miguel told her he had to leave to the office to finish up some of his calls and that he would see her on Monday.

"Sweet Dreams" he wrote at the end of the note.

Miguel quietly placed the note to her side and slipped out of the apartment.

Chapter Twelve
Miguel Dancing Through Time

From that point forward in the year 1998 Beatrice and Miguel had a *dalliance* that lasted two years!

For those two years they made love (or sex as it is often referred): at least twice a week.

Beatrice was an honest gal and used contraceptives.

Miguel felt happy with her: yet he knew that she was not the one for him. Beatrice was *too* demanding in wanting things her way---he felt for her and did love her---but his love was one of friendship.

Toward the end of the relationship of *blissful moments*, Miguel found it necessary to officially end it: Beatrice was becoming more and more *in need* of him as a *soul mate*. Unfortunately, Miguel did not feel the same way.

One night, after a beautiful sexual engagement, Miguel held Beatrice in his arms as both lay on his bed. Miguel then took this opportunity to tell her that their escapades of sexual emotions needed to stop: that this type of free love making had to come to a close because he saw *her pain* of wanting more.

Miguel felt compelled to remind her that their relationship was *pure friendship* and no more.

Miguel told Beatrice that he wanted to keep the friendship that had grown, but that the sexual part needed to end since it was taking her to an emotional level he was not reaching (and a level he had no intentions in reaching).

Beatrice understood, although she became emotionally distraught.

DISTRAUGHT

From that last-sexual-encounter that inspired her for more and more and possibly marriage, those words by Miguel SHATTERED Beatrice to the point of deep depression.

All of Beatrice's aspirations in her mind to move Miguel towards marriage and children came crashing down for Beatrice.

The sting of reality was too great to bear, it did not go unnoticed in her daily routines.

As such, Beatrice made a painful effort to force herself to stay away from Miguel.....as much as possible.

However, the more she left him alone, the more she wanted him!

Wanted Him!

It was a difficult matter for Beatrice in her mind: torn between her wants, needs, and denials.

Beatrice kept a straight face as much as possible.

The dilemma however began building exponentially in her mind...which provoked her to make a permanent separation from Miguel.

Beatrice began to look for employment elsewhere.

On her last day at work, which she had kept secret from everyone in the office, including her reluctant love of her life, Beatrice left Miguel *a note* telling him that her love for him will always be...

...and that she needed to distance herself from him.

She wrote:

"It is hurting me too much; not being able to touch you and feel you inside me. Wanting more than our agreed upon sexual rendezvous...wanting you as my husband. I will always hold you dear to my heart. I wish you always the best always the better."

And with that Beatrice was gone.

Upon reading the note: Miguel felt shameful in assuming that both parties to the *dalliance* were on the same page.

Miguel asked his human-resource accountant to give Beatrice a monthly $16,000 severance pay for the next 7 months as he wanted to make sure that Beatrice's financial situation was not placed in jeopardy from her leaving Miguel's employment.

Miguel wanted to keep in contact with Beatrice...but knew that would only aggravate her...so as much as that friendship meant to him: he had to also deny his wants and needs.

During his beautiful rendezvous time with Beatrice, and before Beatrice's departure, Miguel joined a ballroom dance studio to learn to dance all types of music.

His favorite was Salsa.

Beatrice was not much into dancing and had declined to join Miguel for his weekly dance instruction sessions.

For Miguel, *dance* was an opportunity to be close to women (while not having to make a commitment to any of them). *Dance* was liberating, and the social reward of meeting many different women through *Dance* was wonderful.

In Miguel's mind, *Dance* was a useful tool toward the essence of one's need to be physically close to people.

Miguel was fortunate enough to have women gravitate toward him in a sexual way.

Yet this "fortune" spelled trouble for him after his relationship experience with Beatrice...so he declined sexual advances made toward him...wanting to keep it cordial and fun but no more.

Platonic relationships became his creed again after Beatrice.

If he was going to have sexual relationships he was first going to seek something lasting rather than adventurous.

Miguel told himself that his intent needed to be first love and compatibility rather than having his hormones satisfied...placing them in check: not having them sexually dictate his important decisions.

So, with this in mind, Miguel continued to dance salsa.

The entire dancers at the studio he went to called *Eduardo Caballé Dance Studio* became friends.

The studio emphasized the `conscious` study of synthetic geometric movements in Salsa in order to elaborate further in each movement, and in order to develop complex variety movements within the genre.

This type of `conscious` approach was unique for a dance studio (which is what attracted Miguel to be part of it).

(Miguel operated much of his business using the concepts of synthetic geometry in resolving business issues, expansion, and collaboration for a healthy profit while leaving behind a positive and solid foundation for growth in all that was developed as a consequence to this approach.)

(In a nutshell, Miguel's approach to business was unique!)

Eduardo Caballé Dance Studio was also active in annual dance competitions.

Miguel liked the dance but did not feel *the want* or need to compete with anyone in this form: he wanted to keep it fun.

And so, Miguel went dancing and did occasional exhibitions but entered no competitions---- although he was an endowed and graceful ballroom dancer.

During the time of this dancing era, Miguel moved out of the guest house he had been in since he arrived to California. He decided to make a real-estate purchase other than those made for his businesses.

He purchased a beach-front home in Santa Monica, California... just north of the Santa Monica Pier.

Once the property was purchased, Miguel had the preexisting home torn down in order to build a modern Spanish Style home with three floors and a roof deck with a Jacuzzi.

He also had two indoor car garages built.

A narrow space on one side of the property allowed him to build a small, one-lane, 7 feet deep swimming pool which he used regularly for *muscle* conditioning.

He had his home built to his specifications---from the outside it had a modern feel to it despite being influenced by old Spanish architecture.

However, within its walls it was furnished and decorated in the old colonial Spanish style architecture which was not apparent from looking at the outside.

Miguel had two cars: an S.U.V. and a small two door vehicle. He always updated his cars to the newest year model at the beginning of Valentine's Day!

He opted to purchase the new cars and donate the older ones. He didn't see the logic behind leasing cars and "technically" being in debt to a third party. This is how he ran his business: he would not grow his business unless he had the majority of his *own* capital to invest.

As such, Miguel made it a point to stay away from lending institutions. It made no sense to him to jeopardize ones livelihood at the hands of sharks!

As to his older cars: Miguel would scout the bus stops in search of a family in need. He figured that *direct* support to the needy was best!

Despite the yearly change in cars, Miguel preferred the low profile cars: so he opted for semi luxury cars apart from the German and Italian models. In this way, he thought, he could maintain some sort of normalcy in terms of being able to go outside and not being pegged as someone with wealth.

Keeping a low profile was difficult for Miguel because of his attractive physical features (combined with his sophisticated and elegant manner).

Miguel also had a mystery about him in his *eyes* as someone who liked to explore the *unknown*. This attracted both sexes!

Time had passed quickly for Miguel after his affair with Beatrice.

In fact, seven years rolled by and it became apparent that he needed to settle down; he needed, he felt, to be *less* selfish.

Despite all his business adventures and a good flux of friends, he now felt that he needed a soul mate.

Miguel felt the need to give to someone; and also to have someone that would understand him and see the struggles he never shared with anyone.

Besides, his self-imposed celibacy was now in constant combat with his body's hormones. The body wanted a *healthy* and *regular* passionate tryst with another body or bodies. To spurt out the fruits of life!

sSpurt Out! Spurt Out!

Consequently, Miguel, occupying a biological human body, also had to make some sort of change to feed his body's particular needs!

sex sex sex

On March 17, 2007, Miguel was now a *new* 10 day old *39 years old*!

On that day, Miguel began, as he *assumed*
Beatrice had as well in her past, to seriously
pursue such a person that he thought would be
ideal to understand his inner workings.

Someone who could nurture him in a way that
would help build his soul!

 Miguel began dating weekly in search of the so
called *right* woman for him; He even opted to also
use the Internet dating services to help him find a
soul mate.

After numerous in person conversations and
emails back and forth via the Internet dating
services platform, and his friends'
recommendations, it was apparent to Miguel that
this task was not going to be easy.

 His physical preferences as to race were open: he
found *all* women of all ethnicities and races
beautiful. Each one had their unique way of
expressing themselves. Miguel had no prejudices
in this regard.

Yet, none of the women he began dating had the
compatibility he was looking for: a combination
of intellectual and emotional nurturing support.

After two months of unsuccessful soul mate searching, Miguel began to think that maybe his frame of mind was wrong; he began to think that maybe he was being too picky!

picky picky picky

At the end of August 15, 2007, Miguel had not found *The One*. So he decided to stop this exhausting activity and just continue to focus on his businesses. He had learned that "being pushy" was not good in any endeavor.

in any endeavor.

ErgO, Miguel decided to practice patience and to let fate takes its course. If he found *The One* then he would be happy. If he didn't find *The One*, then life would go on and he would find other things to keep him motivated.

Besides, Miguel enjoyed his work. Business for him was an *art form* which he gradually learned to perfect.

Miguel had associates for each of his companies of which he shared this art form stage! Although the companies were wholly his, Miguel's approach to issues and innovation within his businesses were always team work.

If he didn't see an adequate solution, one of his team members would after debriefings and spending long hours or days coming up with the best solutions. It was a reciprocal relationship in terms of growing and operating a business...like the communications done between neurons!... Equal footing to send signals to the appropriate locations!

Miguel paid his associates more than most big corporate companies do...AND an additional little more!

His appreciative compensation to the beneficial help from his entire work force was enormous.

Through his direct guidance and vision, the companies prospered **BIG!**

Miguel was easy to get along with, and most people that met him liked him *immediately.*

Keeping it real and being kind were and are his natural traits and this appealed greatly to all people.

Chapter Thirteen
Jana and Miguel: The Beginning Of A Wonderful Relationship

And so on that faithful day of September 12, 2007, Miguel found what he was looking for in the person named Jana.

Fates joined together into something that was *destined*.

As they walked back from the beach, Miguel's new home overlooking the ocean was impressive to look at: a mostly Spanish style modern design from the outside. The feel *within* it had the smell and look of a long-ago Spanish Villa when the colonies of Mexico were run by the dignitaries of Spain.

And California was the furthest, outermost colony of Spain...part of an envisioned empire that eventually would be transferred by *a mediator* into the hands of the newly formed world empire (the Jewish state called The United States of America).

This was Miguel's home; a home he knew unconsciously was only for a *designated time*...a time preceding a bigger purpose.

The *Love Birds* entered into Miguel's large bedroom which had a huge bathroom.

As both entered dancing a waltz of kisses and touches...each could taste and feel the salt water on their lips of the other.

Suddenly, as if something different, the Love Birds just held each other in-STILLness.

...shoulder to shoulder: *breathing deeply* but deeply not of lust or desire but

of relief

of inspiration

of Hope and Faith!

Both Love Birds felt something special in this newly formed Union. It was not like any other union they had *ever* felt before.

Something was different.

Something was very different!

Miguel felt that he had finally found the love of his life.

And Jana felt *secure* in his arms.

It felt to Jana as if she had known Miguel *all her life*.

And, it felt to Jana that she had finally been able to physically *grasp* this man who brought her peace.

Perhaps Miguel was a long lost image she had created for the *man of her dreams*.

...or perhaps Miguel was Pli multe.

...or perhaps Miguel was *Máis*.

...or perhaps Miguel was *more*!

...a being that Jana had reached for in the past but that which was *like a ghost* she couldn't hold.

Jana had tried and tried to reach for him in the past; but only in her mind was she able to do that.

And now, *finally*, the man of her dreams and of much much more had *materialized*!

Happiness prevailed for that moment that had eluded both of them up to this point in time; not the happiness of partying or of sex or of companionship.

Rather, it was something *special* which both could *not put into words*; it was something new; yet something familiar.

Both stood holding each other for a good *f i v e* minutes; both with their eyes closed.

The *mantra* breathing continued in them and between them!

Both seemed *asleep*.

What broke the Union was Jana's dropping to the side; *she was asleep*!

Miguel quickly held her tight so as not to let her fall.

She slowly opened her eyes and looked at Miguel.

Not a word was said; *not a word.*

Miguel gently released Jana after a few moments had passed and led her to the spacious walk-in shower room; which was beautifully adorned with dark brown marble.

Both stood beneath the motionsless shower head which had two marble like planks which released the water.

The shower stood at the center of the room, curtainless.

Jana felt drowsy...but with each new breath...she was beginning to feel revived (and excitement began to stir within her).

At the center of the spacious bathroom, Miguel gently raised her hands, reached for her brassiere and unlaced it.

Miguel then unbuttoned her blouse and gently lifted the brassiere and blouse together.

Moving his hands down to her hips he STOPPED and *breathed in* the view: "Oh what beautiful, lushes breasts and hips she has", Miguel thought.

He unbuttoned her skirt and pulled them down along with her wet underwear.(Miguel felt his erection beginning to tighten!)

Her pubic hair was a beautiful light brown *red*. It seemed like it had never been shaved—it was such a beautiful bush (fluffy and lovely and not trimmed!...POSING THERE in its natural array!). [man did Miguel love that natural look!]

Then it was *her* turn; Jana reached for Miguel's diver type trunks and *gently* and *slowly* pulled them down. Miguel's erection was growing: It was long and dark. Jana gently stroked it. She felt it harden. Jana gracefully *bent down* and *slowly* kissed it.

Miguel lowered his arms and touched her shoulder with his hands. Jana stood *knelt* and kissed it more.

After a *good* while, she then gracefully stood up and kissed his chin.

Miguel looked down at Jana's beautiful *face* and kissed it: first in the *forehead*, then on her *nose*, then on her right *cheek*!

Miguel paused and took a deep *breath of her* face in a circular motion until he reached her left *cheek* and gently kissed it.

He took a *good* while to remove his lips from her left *cheek* (it was as though he was communicating with her from *within*).

communicating.

Finally, Miguel slightly bent his knees and kissed her lips with a *gentleness* and *commitment* that would make butterflies look ridiculous!

Miguel reached out to turn the water on; it ran cold at first on his back, then it quickly became warm. He reacted to the cold water as it hit his back.

When Miguel felt the water was warm, he turned Jana toward it. The warm water slowly rinsed the salts from their bodies.

On the ground next to them was a basket with sponges. Miguel took a large oval *soft sponge* and added water and a bar of fragrant soap creating foam by rubbing them together.

Miguel carefully and very diligently cleansed every part of Jana's body. At least he thought he had!

Miguel realized he had forgotten *one spot*.

He gently began to separate her legs; Jana helped by moving one leg apart.

He cleaned her gently; Jana felt safe with Miguel.

Jana did not know what was going to happen next although she imagined that he would enter her shortly.

After rinsing her and shampooing and conditioning her hair; Jana replied in kind— Miguel loved feeling her soft, long fingers caress his body.

As Jana shampooed Miguel's hair...he gently kissed her arms...one and then the other.

Not a word was said.

Each dried the other with the same towel and rubbed the head of the other to dry the hairs.

It was a moment to be remembered; a moment that both felt in the past would possibly never come.

It had arrived.

Miguel was happy; Jana was happy. The time had arrived for both of them to be *uniquely* happy; a time that some are not as fortunate to experience in a lifetime.

Miguel led Jana back into the bedroom toward the *king* size plush bed.

Jana sat down at the side of the bed as Miguel knelt down in front of her.

The passion was instantaneous.

They embraced each other and kissed fervently.

With *increased* excitement, Jana laid back on the bed and placed her head on a pillow: prompting Miguel *onto* her.

They kissed for a good while.

Jana felt the strength of his penis on her thigh.

She wanted him so badly/ she wanted him *inside* her!

Her inner vagina moistened rapidly.

Jana waited for Miguel to *enter* her.

She *waited*!

Miguel lowered his head to kiss every part of her body.

Jana lay surprised at his *patience* not to *penetrate* her.

As Miguel reached her groin, he kissed her thighs; one and then the other.

Miguel lowered himself more and more until he had reached Jana's heels. He caressed them with his cheeks, stroking them oh-ever-*so gently*.

This unknown `action` in her life aroused her even more!

Miguel then proceeded to move upward.

...gently separating Jana's legs and holding them near his earlobes with his hands.

Miguel lowered his head and kissed Jana's outer lobes (her labia *majoras*)

Majoras!

He then gently probed them with his tongue.

The penetration with his tongue continued into-her labia minoras.

Minoras!

Finally Miguel stroked Jana's clitoris with his lips and tongue...leaving behind a slue of saliva as if prepping it for excitement!

The motion of his lips and tongue created a smooth-synchronized-rhythm.

Synchronized!

Smooth!

Rhythm!

They were a team.

　　　　　　...a team of pleasure!

An *experienced* team of pleasure!

Jana was about to explode!

Jana wanted to clasp her legs *tightly* around Miguel's head...she refrained.

Jana tried hard to control her urges.

She held the **deniance** at bay!

...suffering her **denied-desires** in hopes of something better.

Better!

[this is pretty good! pretty better!]

But it seemed that her legs had other plans:

...Jana's ground-limbs began applying light pressure to Miguel's shoulders.

She was *losing* control over her body.

[the human body designed to follow foremost the instructions of the proteins rather than that of the *energy* within...]

[...that *eternal energy* trapped within the encasement; controlled by the encasement and those that rule the environment of the encasement!].

Miguel *gently* raised his head and *gently* lowered her legs.

Slowly Miguel climbed further until his head reached hers.

Whispering Miguel said, "You are *so* beautiful".

Jana was flattered.

Jana lifted her head slightly requesting a kiss.

Miguel delivered a passionate *long* one.

As they kissed Jana could *not hold* not control herself any longer:

Jana spread her legs apart further and pleaded with her hips for his penetration.

Miguel lowered his hips and grabbed his penis and penetrated Jana.

Jana moaned and *exhaled* a long-loud cry.

The sound aroused Miguel as he felt Jana's hands clasp his buttocks and push him toward her *even more*.

Every stroke brought forward a moan from Jana.

It seems as if she was dying.

Her screams became *louder* and *louder*.

and *louder* and *louder*.

and *louder* and *louder*.

Miguel breathed heavily as he penetrated her continuously and faster at each insertion.

Miguel created deliberate and consistent motions-on-*the ascend*.

Miguel tried desperately not to *come*, he tried to focus on not *coming*.

Miguel began to breathe more in order to monitor his *coming*.

...but Jana's **exhibited-excitement** *overpowered* Miguel.

...he began to moan and moan *louder* like never before.

...Jana felt Miguel was about to *come*.

She had *come* once in the beginning before he penetrated her; then again as he thrust himself into her.

Jana was **exalted** to a *realm-of-disbelief.*

She wanted *more!*

Miguel began to *come (*while simultaneously sensing Jana still had not climaxed to her *full* potential: so he held back once more...although some semen had escaped his control).

This conscious action by Miguel excited Jana *even more* to the point of no return.

Miguel noticed her *coming.*

Miguel accordingly thrust himself deeper and deeper and *came in her.*

... pronouncing a yell of a non-human language...it was completely uncontrollable and spontaneous.

Miguel *held it in her*.

After a good thirty-four seconds, Miguel slowly slid his penis out and immediately re-thrust it into her once more in slow motion.

(...there appeared to be a liquid-thread connecting them...for that moment an unbreakable liquid-thread of Jana and Miguel held!).

Miguel was *utterly* spent.

Jana held him as he lowered his head to her side.

Jana wanted Miguel *inside her*.

The tension within her had receded. Jana *felt his softness*...his innocence.

If Jana had a choice, she would want Miguel *inside her always*.

With her hands, she gently held his buttocks.

Jana gracefully kissed Miguel's neck.

This was the *best* sex she had *ever* felt!!!

For the first time in Jana's life it felt like "*love making*".

Jana cared for Miguel (a deep-felling to love without explanation or condition)... despite knowing very little of him.

Something stirred in the **unknown** inside her which was growing in-intensity and power, which had no explanation or understanding except to love him unconditionally...as a child loves a loved one.

There existed at that moment a *wordless* communication that *told her* Miguel was for her and she for him.

A bold mental statement, subconsciously Jana doubted as a bad habit, but she didn't care.

Jana began from that moment *to trust* her senses:

those-supernatural-eternal-senses that are practiced little in society.

...a society that apparently seems to intentionally distract one **from** connecting to one's eternity.

Odd.

Why the intentional distractions by those rulers of the human conscious?

Jana lay there pondering this question.

Miguel lightly slept on Jana while his left shoulder leaned against the bed; he did not want to apply too much pressure on her as he slept.

Jana too *slowly* fell asleep.

...feeling his penis still inside her.

She smiled as she dozed off into another reality.

Jana slept and slept and slept.

And slept and slept.

When Jana woke she had covers over her.

Miguel was not there.

At the bed's side table, Miguel had left a folded note with *a rose*. Jana leaned to open it. It read:

"*I wish I was still here with you; had to go to work to take care of some errands. Please sleep more. Take your time. There is food in the refrigerator. I'll see you at 4 p.m. If you can wait for me, I will be very pleased. But, if you need to go, I'll understand.*

With a passionate kiss,

Miguel."

The note was dated Thursday, September 13, 2007. The clock displayed a time of 7:30 a.m.

Jana smelled the card and smiled.

After a good while of drifting into a day dream, Jana breathed deeply, swayed to her left, and placed the note back onto the table.

Jana had scheduled herself to start her school prep week at 10:00 a.m. to avoid traffic. She had time to *breath*.

This school year Jana had modified her availability in order to spend more time to know herself. Jana committed in advance in only teaching four periods per day ending by 2:05 p.m. This flex schedule would provide her with time to do her planning, grading, and other course preparations earlier and be ready for self-analysis by 4 p.m.

Today though was completely unexpected...her conscious self-analysis of her person was thrown

out the window*!*

Jana lay back and thought of *positive feelings*.

Those thoughts weren't self-analysis.

Jana *thought* and *thought* and *thought*.

The images in her mind were beautiful: images of complete *peace*...this feeling existing inside her that very moment! Oh it felt so good. Good!

Felt so good.

A peace that *aligned* how every **bit of her** felt: *a meaningful purpose*.

"¡Qué lindo!" She said in her mind. "Nunca me he sentido ¡con tanta paz!".

Jana's mind then TRANSFORMED her images into the images of the beauty of the people of Guadalajara.

Jana remembered when she went there in her past for a four year study of the Spanish language.

Jana's desire was to be the best in what she taught.

And with this objective in mind: going to an environment where Spanish was prominent was exactly what she needed to meet that goal.

Much of her time there was spent at the surrounding universities: gaining academic knowledge of the linguistic exploration of the language and its variants.

And for the varied multi-faceted cultures existing within Mexico, Jana took every opportunity to visit every single part of Mexico....to mingle with the people...to learn their ways.

This exploration instilled in Jana a strong desire to someday *meet* someone as a significant-other from this land of Mestizos (the *beauty* of the integration of the European and Native American blood that had been made there since before 1492).

Even though Jana meet many handsome men during her stay in Mexico including in the regions of Guadalajara, Mexico City (D.F.), and elsewhere, she refrained from pursuing any of them.

In her mind **back then** Jana felt she needed to create A SELF-IMPOSED-DISCIPLINE in order to successfully achieve her goal: taking the time in Mexico ONLY for the *pure*-purpose of successfully acquiring the language to-beyond an academic fluency (and nothing more).

So with that `limiting frame-of-mind,` Jana hesitated and halted all obvious proposals she received from men while in Mexico.

These men understood her explanation and accepted and respected her decision.

Although in reality she found it very very difficult inside to say no...she needed someone...she desired someone...and here in the *land of enchantment* existed these *precious beings*. Jana so desired them...their easy way of life mentality, not double or triple faced like in the United States, and their physical features were compelling and difficult to veer one's eyes away from.

Now in retrospect, *on this morning* in Miguel's home, Jana saw this past restrictive thinking as dumb: **the University of California at Los Angeles** created this rigidity in her human mind that was contagious for a student who wanted to succeed in life.

"¡Que mensa!", she thought.

But everything has a reason for existing and so this is what became of her life...stuck in a job teaching Spanish whose administrators respected educators little: always finding ways of extracting from them and retaining the benefits of monetary compensation for themselves.

In this morning moment though, Jana's *mind* was not remotely near any type of negativity.

Jana **lay** still in a man's bed...

a man's bed*!*

She smiled.

Jana had made a *close connection* to someone special in this **lonesome** world of uncertainties.

Jana felt a **blanket of love** embrace her at the thought of this *close connection* experience.

Stretching her feet, Jana turned around in her tummy and closed her eyes.

Quickly she fell asleep.

Jana dreamt and dreamt not *remembering* nothing of what she was seeing---all she could feel at this moment was a *sigh of relief* from all the turmoil her life had gone through. She felt free. ...free to sleep!

free *to be* *free!*

PART 3 of 7
A MIXTURE OF PLEASURE AND PAIN

Chapter Fourteen
A Proposition

When Jana returned to Miguel's home from work she was surprised by a smile on the driveway.

It was 3:45 in the afternoon and Miguel had just pulled up to the driveway. Jana placed her car in an empty space next to Miguel's.

As Jana stepped-out of her car she was received by a gentle-moistened kiss to her lips.

Jana felt the warmness and softness of the kiss and *took it in* with all her being.

The moments that followed were like a dream where everything flowed with the sound of a continuous *rhythm*: both beings *together* and *harmoniously* talked, made love, showered, and breathed in the *air of contentment*.

air of contentment

They talked about each other and both were happy to be free *to be together*.

To Be Together

The discussions ranged from their occupations, dreams, tragedies, and Hope and Faith for the future.

Miguel expressed his desire to make their relationship **regular** and **ongoing**.

...In so many cues Miguel was making Jana a PROPOSITION.

He wanted her as his wife but without all the legal garbage.

Both Jana and Miguel had come to realize that they both wanted a *pure love* free of restrictive cultural confinements.

..away from those **Meddlers!**:

"**D**eceptively **T**actful **M**eddlers" (**DTMs**) who placed it in their minds that they owned you! But as to ownership, there is only One: GOD of the Jews...not the self-imposed caretakers...mere lost energies wanting to grow and to have their false god grow!

...Worshipers of the Sun.

In their minds the **Meddlers** see the masses in that way: forcefully placing a **nine**-digit-number tag to each human being at birth, writing a certificate of death at the bodily departure of the encased energy... and the garbage goes on and on.

Yes on and on...the **9**-Digit-Pushers (**9**-DPs)...

Egyptianizing everything down to the last molecule!

One organization with many faces...the same thing... **9-DPs**

- - -

As the discussions continued, both Jana and Miguel acknowledged and informed the other that there were things in their past that they had not resolved in their minds: very intimate issues that still caused pain in their minds, and pasts that still shaped their habits...both good ones and uncomfortable ones.

The **𝕴**nter**m**ingling **𝕭**ird**s** (IBs) agreed that sensitive issues that were *melancholic* in one way or another were *not acceptable to continue* in their daily lives.

...and that the negative habits they formed were slowly but surely being exterminated from daily use.

Many things in their pasts however were not *fully* understood on a conscious or unconscious level: and that those required more reflection and sharing to identify and eliminate.
Both agreed to help each other in resolving those difficult **t**riangles-**o**f-**u**nspecified-**c**oordinates (**TOUC**s).

Miguel stressed this importance of "*collaboration*" to Jana as if leading it to some conclusion:

Miguel shared with Jana that "imperfections" in their own persons needed to be let go of *completely* in their minds in order to truly grow and become more fulfilled and happy as human beings.

Jana agreed fully with Miguel (although she felt she had more hang-ups than Miguel...seeing some sort of imbalance).

In his proposition to her, Miguel *invited* Jana to take time off from her regular job and have time to *explore* all those past events that kept her unfulfilled.

A Free Pass He Could Afford For Her.

Sagaciously and Sagaciously in Congruency, the couple knew that an exclusive "loving" relationship with another human being was not "suffice" for the complete-fulfillment-of-a-person in its growth towards complete self-realization.

Due to the *limitations of being a human,* finding closure to uncertainties towards a peaceful medium requires bringing into fruition COMPONENTS beyond just loving another human being or human beings.

...it is essential to practice deep reflection in the analysis of oneself...an opposite movement from the tangling-environments that distracts our attention away from making the GENUINE-TIME toward the tasks of obtaining true and eternal self-fulfillment and knowledge and awareness.

Gripping COMPONENTS that encompass peace, contentment, realization, empowerment, and a purposeful-and-meaningful **intent** toward an eternal direction is what is needed.

And so here was Jana.

...Thinking about Miguel's proposition.

Was Jana really not going to work and have time she never had before to think and think and relax?

Jana kissed Miguel on the forehead and said,

"Let's have breakfast".

Breakfast at 5 p.m. in the afternoon sounded marvelous to her.

"I'll make you breakfast here in your house."

Miguel *gracefully* took her hand and said:

"Our house".

Jana walked silently as Miguel held her hand. They both headed toward the kitchen.

Miguel offered to help but Jana wanted to serve him for this special occasion.

After she cooked and served the food (over and easy eggs, white toast, milk, and orange juice), Jana made a gesture to Miguel with her hands.

Making a circular motion she said:

"Listen Miguel, I will accept your offer if I can be like a house-wife who prepares food for her working Husband."

Miguel softly reached and touched her hands and said, "No."

"Mi amor: quiero que tu seas libre sin ningún compromiso de hacerme nada."

He translated it into English, forgetting that Jana was fluent in the Spanish language:

"I want you to be free without any obligations of any sort".

He went on:

"I want you to relax and be *free to complete yourself.*"

"So.....please accept my offer without any obligations."

"I will handle all of your finances as you explore your *true self*----I'll cover your rent and other items. And even if this relationship at the end does not work out---you owe me *no obligation.*"

This detailed proposition made Jana nervous.

No one had ever offered to help her in such a profound way.

Jana breathed deeply and silently...she was working hard in her mind to overcome her anxiety at such a proposition.

Jana did want desperately to be different—she wanted a *real turn* in her life and thus concluded that she needed to trust Miguel.

trust.

Jana needed to trust fate regardless of where it may turn.

Jana *slowly* reached over the small wooden table, kissed Miguel *softly* on the lips, and nodded a

"*yes!*"

Chapter Fifteen
Intensification Of The Dream

The first weeks with Miguel were wonderful!

Miguel showed Jana the **dance life**...both taking Salsa lessons (even though he was already fluent in this dance form).

Jana became quite competent despite missteps in the beginning. Like all new activities, one learns with practice: and practice they did!

Every weekend they took the opportunity to show their coordinated rhythmic **motions** in public.

During the week they rehearsed at home to the point where both were drenched in sweat!

Sweat!!!

Dance provided them a medium of expression like no other physical activity.

If truly executed with sincere intent, the outcome becomes an expression of one's inner self*!*

And when the dance entails two or more beings, it provides the extra benefit of learning to communicate with another human being without words.

Without words!

A non-human action!

 Isn't that wonderful!?

...becoming an expert to competently communicate with another human being without words.

Without words!

...leaving culture to its culture and being able to exercise *eternity*!

No restrictions of mind, body, or energy.

 Pure intent*!*

pure existence!

No nos and no yaees.

No good and no "bad".

pure indulgence no restrictions.

When time permitted, Jana and Miguel traveled throughout California exploring the mountains, coasts, and desserts together.

Miguel showed Jana her first cultural encounters of San Francisco.

Miguel loved the people there: they didn't seem as pretentious as in Los Angeles. They seemed to be okay to be themselves at the moment...regardless of their social, cultural, ethnic, racial, or financial status.

Miguel had so much fun in San Francisco that he had strong considerations of moving there.

Miguel was actually preparing plans of opening another plant there, and in opening a second base of operations there as well: making it possible to reside there more regularly.

More regularly!

Miguel was grateful that he had not yet made that move! If he had, he probably would not have met Jana.

So fate had a hand in withholding the plan.

Miguel smiled.

The ports of Los Angeles and San Francisco offered his business a great place to distribute his Mexican wares that came from all parts of Mexico: including from his bakery factories in Mexico City.

"Maybe-one-day", he thought, "vamos a ver, algún día iré a San Francisco a vivir...pero ahora cuando lo haga, lo haré con mi amor eterna: la mujer de mis sueños: Jana."

In her new life, Jana was able to sleep.

Her dreams were pleasant.

Miguel always awoke quietly in the morning; not wanting to wake Jana.

Jana was grateful at his considerations not only of this but in alternating with her in cooking dinner.

An activity that both found therapeutic...creating and sharing the creation!

Miguel truly knew how to cook well: and he did it with such patience that it astonished Jana.

Jana had never met a man with *so much patience.*

One day when Jana rose from her sleep, an idea came to her mind:

"**Write a story!**", Jana said aloud to herself.

"...get a pen and paper and **write a story!**"

Jana didn't quite know just what type of story it would be; but she felt a need (`a drive`) to write in hopes that she would be able to explore and better understand her *inner workings*.

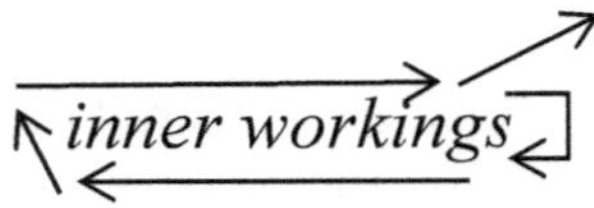

Jana supposed that everyone shared the same plight of the unknown about WHO WE REALLY ARE.

Jana was determined to write to see what **fruition-of-realization** would be revealed to her: maybe a glimpse into other realms of reality (or realities) or an understanding of our human condition or maybe even more!

On Monday morning, late November 2007, while she returned from her morning run, Jana noticed a change in her mood.

The running was not helping her cope with her anxieties that seemed to be growing inside her.

"Maybe it's the cold air that is affecting me", she thought. "Maybe I need to run later."

As Jana entered the beach-front home, she involuntarily collapsed to the ground onto her knees feeling nauseated.

Jana had this great sensation of throwing up""7

Jana forced herself up and headed to the bathroom in the hall.

But after a few steps she threw up""7...

...expelling ""'"".........all of the well-liquefied foods from her stomach onto

the.....marble floor...............................

Immediately after the food fell on the ground, Jana followed with her body onto the hard marble.

Jana desperately attempted to outreach with her hands to break the fall as she headed (face down) toward the floor.

The slow motion view looked as if her body was in rhythmic unison with her vomit

Despite her hands breaking some of the fall, Jana did hit her forehead with a good amount of force.

f or ce

Jana ricocheted abruptly from the floor: creating an inaudible-sound-sensation within her.

When her head landed again onto the floor, Jana tried not to move for fear of injuring herself even more.

Her hands desperately gripped the slippery floor.

The room seemed to spin around her and she felt like she was mounted-on-a-**spindle** that would *not stop*!

Not Stop!

Jana painfully moaned loudly...**eking** out her frustrations *audibly*.

Jana decided not to move at all...resting her face on the floor.

After several minutes, Jana noticed that she was on-her-own-*vomit*

Jana was struggling to breath.

At that moment she breathed heavily: inhaling some of her vomit and coughing it out. She stayed their half-asleep, as if she were drunk.

Jana found herself in an undesirable place where she did not have the strength to pick herself up from from the "**SH I T**" beneath her and on her and in her/

As time elapsed slowly, Jana began losing more and more strength.

The *intensity* of her physical state OVercame her, and Jana completely collapsed unconscious onto the FLOOR.

After an ***uncountable*** segment-of-time, Jana opened her eyes.

Everything was dark around her.

The doors had disappeared and Jana now found herself on *fertile* soil.

As Jana stood up she noticed she was completely naked and her hair had grown longer than it was (it reached to her waist!).

The hair's texture was thick and black.

Jana then looked at her skin and it was not light brown but dark brown.

Jana then probed her face, feeling a change in it. After removing the dirt she felt on her face, Jana noticed the extra prominent check bones on her face.

Although she was able to see at a close distance of 2 feet, everything further than this was in darkness:

Jana saw nothing but darkness!

2 feet further Jana heard horse hoofs trampling the ground---pacing slowly and then fast and then slowly again.

Jana suddenly felt a strong-decisive breeze around her hair.

After *taking in* this physical phenomenon, Jana realized that it was not *wind-breeze* but that of something **breathing down on** her.

This current of air was warm and moist.

Jana SLO W L Y turned around and found the source of this *breeze*.

As she turned, Jana saw a tall dark-skin man standing directly behind her.

Jana had to lift her face up to gaze at this man's face who was looking *onwards*.

The man spoke!:

"Look!"

He lifted his hand and pointed forward.

"Look Shesha"

"There!", he pointed.

"There you will find *life* that will bring warmth to us all."

Jana turned around to where the man was pointing and all of a sudden she noticed an open space of land:

A *Vibrant* Land!

...Green pastures of small hills...as far as the naked eye can see...for miles and miles.

Jana did not know at first what this man was telling her. The man spoke another language (a non-English and a non-Spanish language) and yet she understood him. However, the man was talking about foreign themes Jana knew nothing about.

Instinctively, Jana closed her eyes and breathed in deeply....as if looking for something.

Jana continued to breath with her eyes closed...she breathed in something familiar and yet unfamiliar.

Jana's nostrils picked up a scent of fur and dirt.

f u r   a n d   d i r t

In her *inner-most* part-of-her-being there existed a prior consciousness Jana knew nothing about.

Yet this DATA within her became understandable after a few *time lapses*.

Jana began to recognize the smell:

B U F F A L O

B U F F A L O

B U F F A L O

Jana's SENSE OF SMELL opened up in such a way as never before!

This long ago consciousness (existing before the Jana of now) had been restored!

Jana was immediately able to identify the scent-of-present.

Jana opened her eyes again and there in the distant American plains...*far far away*...she saw small **spots** of dark brown.

It was almost sunset.

Almost *Sunset*!

SOLENS DOMMEDAG!

Jana knew that the hunt for buffalo was also conducted during the shaded-hours-of-the-day.

During the night hunt the sense of smell predominated all-other-human-Senses.

The Warrior's skills on the procedure to accurately and efficiently bring down a huge beast (being the American Buffalo) (without getting killed) were-well-rehearsed.

WELL-REHEARSED

Only the keenest hunters were used during these night hunts.

Keenest was Key!

Key Keenest!

Skarpeste Er Nøglen

Nøglen Er Skarpeste

Top notch warriors were needed for this invisible-display of amazing marksmanship and equestrian mastery.

"Shesha, mount your horse and ride with us," the same *voice* behind her urged her.

"Your spear is on the horse waiting for you. Go out and conquer what is yours!"

"Go out and *be free* to be Shesha."

"You've been away so long from us and now the God of all has brought you back to us."

"Go out and fulfill your destiny."

"Go out Shesha and be one with the land; be one with your tribe."

Jana sensed the horse that bore-her-mark.

Jana sprang around the corner of were the man stood: sensing her horse.

She reached out and clasped the **mane-of-the-horse** until she had completely swung her entire body *on-t*op-of-the-Stallion.

Jana kicked the horse with the heel of her naked feet and grunted the horse **ONWARD**.

ONWARD

ONWARD

JAMES ALLEN WHITMORE 1921

Immediately, the horse responded.

It **SPED FORWARD** in *lightning speed.*

Jana held on tight to the mane (lowering her head to allow the *wind-space* to bypass her **stride**).

Jana's entire body felt the excitement of the catch to come.

Jana's bow and arrows were securely attached to the horse in a pouch made of buffalo skin.

Jana gently caressed the tip of the arrows and occasionally clasped the side-edge of the arrows with the upper part of her fingers: feeling the collide of her flesh and nails as they applied *tender* pressure.

tender pressure

As Jana neared the catch to come, she saw her brethren, who were crouched at a short distance from the herd of buffalo, ready for the attack.

When they saw her approaching: they *LEAPED* to their horses and headed toward the beasts.

In precise synchronicity, Jana now Shesha met them: and the chase was oN*!* oN*!*   oN*!*

The buffalo raced away toward safety: but the *t*ribe-*O*f-*t*welve warriors encircled them.

e n c i r c l e d   en_{cir}cled .

Each displayed its bow and shot without a moment's wait. They targeted two buffalo--six to a beast.

six-two

six-two

six-two

The beasts resisted but the shot to the spinal cord
of one of the beast quickly paralyzed-its-quick-
movements into

in**stant**-l_im_{ps}.

l_im_{ps}...

... l_im_{ps}

Then it was Jana's spear-headed arrow that drove
itself into the neck of the other beast.

Quickly Shesha jumped on this beast with her ax

in hand: a**X**ing and a**X**ing and a**X**ing the beast
until it fell and came to *a calm.*

a calm

a calm   [you can take the flesh but not the soul! Amén to the
Lord.]

Blood rose to Shesha's face. Feeling *the warmth:*
she **bathed** in it.   **bathed**

bathed

The other five warriors quickly followed up to the animal and finished it off.

All the while, the other injured beast resisted relinquishing-its9earthly-life:

It kept up its fight. It refused to die.

...to die to die [what a lie]

This beast...instead of slowing down after being shot with three arrows to the neck: sped faster and faster and faster!

Jana quickly jumped back on her horse and veered straight toward the runaway beast.

                           r

r una   una   runa

SheSHA quickly caught up to it and jumped on its back: pounding the beast with her ax to its neck

                 neck

                     neck!

The beast DID-NOT Slow until the *seventh*
penetration of her ax reached its neck's **p**rimal-
point
     point
       point

With that irreversible-_{pen}**e**tration: the beast went
head-first straight into a dive: flipping over and
tossing Jana forward.

As Jana fell to the ground, tumbling forward,
sheSHA saw the beast's body crashing toward her
own.

With quick reflexes THIS WOMAN attempted to
move away FROM-THE impending-weight-of-
the-beast.

Jana managed to move-enough-space to avoid the
bulk-of-the-weight-of-the-beast to land
completely on her.

Despite the quickness of this young woman,
Shesha was not able to avoid her limbs from
taking some of the weight.

As the *beast* squirmed dying on the ground, Jana desperately tried to move away.

Her left arm was caught up (to nearly her shoulder) to the *beast*.

Entangled   Ensnarled
Entombed

Entangled   Ensnarled
Entombed

Entangled   Ensnarled
Entombed

The Woman had managed to take her left leg out from under the *beast* but nothing more...she was wounded.

She exhaled a-low- s low-cry-of-PAIN.

Jana was not able to see nothing but the darkness

of the beast's fur on her *face*

face *face*.

Voices approached from a distance and they
muttered words Jana could not understand.

...everything seemed blurred; all her senses came
and went in **milli-segments-of-time**: creating
dizziness in her.

faintness

frailness

failiness

SheSHA tried DILIGENTLY to understand the approaching voices.

Suddenly the injured woman saw a flash of white light and then more flashes and then she woke and found herself being pulled from the ground-of-

vOmit by hands she **still** could not see.

Miguel was speaking to her but Jana could not understand what he was saying—*half of her* was still with the tribe.

When Jana completely entered into the consciousness of the present she **immediately felt** a **huge** disappointment... having tasted a reality she whole-heartedly connected to; something beyond-her-current-dimensional-**station-in-time**.

dimensional-**station-in-time**.

station-in-time

Jana wanted to *stay* with the tribe: **in it***!*

stay ***stay*** ***stay*** and not go.

Jana found purpose in her life---for the first time she felt *purpose* **BEYOND** the *Western* world; an experience Feeza Jana had not lived before; a reality that commanded her presence in the survival of a people of *long ago*.

Jana did not express her disappointment verbally: but Miguel was able to see **THAT** disappointment in her face (filled with vomit **goo goo goo**): her first *response-reaction* back into this reality.

Miguel did not want to question her but help her. After a while: Jana did hear his words:

"Dear, are you alright?*!*".

      "Dear, are you alright?*!*".

"Dear, are you alright?*!*".

After a long while of no response, Jana slowly nodded a "yes".

Chapter Sixteen
The Unexpected News

Miguel carefully lifted Jana from the ground to his arms. He headed to the bathroom when suddenly Jana gripped him ever so tightly; a grip of intensity; a grip of **TENSION!**

"Please, stop." she told him.

Miguel stopped and stood still as Jana held him tightly in her **GRASP**.

Jana neared Miguel's ear and said, "*I love you* Miguel." It was more of a *whisper* than a said.

Miguel understood Jana was under some sort of shock. Miguel understood her **EVEN-THOUGH** he had never experienced this before.

Deep-down-inside Miguel knew he needed to be *patient*.

And he *was*.

Miguel held Jana tight and replied softly, "*sweet-heart*...[he looked deeply into her eyes].... I love you no matter what."

"Can I take you to the bathroom to clean you up?"

Jana responded:

 "My love, please sit on the floor with me. I want to share my dr*eam* with you."

Both sat where Miguel had stood:

right on the floor.

Jana *recited* all that she saw from her dream-experience.

Jana explained to Miguel that she **had had** a previous introduction to this vision.....a vision that brought her **purpose**; a **purpose** of something beyond the now; a **purpose** that lead her toward connecting in a way to *dearly* understanding her **origins**.

"**Vision**", she said. "I am not sure what the word '**Vision**' entails"... "if I somehow transported into this reality." "I felt the breeze Miguel, I felt the lifts, I felt the sm*ell!*"

Jana disclosed further to Miguel some of the reasons for her unhappiness before they met; and how this **Vision** was providing *twinklings* of Hope and Faith in a life she concluded was void of true meaning in her innermost-being; a *yearning* seeking to be filled. [the Merrikis]

Jana explained to Miguel her Native American roots; her Comanche heritage: and how there

existed *voids of information* due to her limited physical contact *with her* father and his people.

... And how her father had left when she was a child and and and

Miguel sat still; listening; not commenting; just listening.

Jana appreciated his attentiveness...even in the face of vomit smell!

After Jana had concluded all what was on her mind to share (a good 25 minutes of it!):

Miguel responded.

"Sweet heart, I am happy you are coming to understand your purpose."

"I cannot say much to you now except: keep on this *journey* of discovery; a *journey* that is taking you to where you belong; a *journey* that is bringing you closer to who you are."

Jana smiled.

Miguel slowly stood up and held out his hand to Jana.

They both went into the wash room where Miguel gently helped bathe her.

Jana did feel weak (and Miguel knew it!).

Something **physical** was going on with Jana.

After the wash Miguel led Jana to the kitchen. They both sat down at the chairs of the small wooden table.

Miguel made her chamomile tea and then proceeded to clean up the floor.

"I will make you an appointment with my doctor tomorrow morning," Miguel said as he cleaned.

Jana nodded yes and *sipped* her tea.

The next morning, Jana was at the medical plaza of Saint John's Hospital.

Dr. Alfredo Ramirez's office was on the 7rd floor.

Jana waited. She looked around the waiting room and appreciated the beautiful view of its surroundings.

Jana felt very pleasant: enjoying the quietness and spaciousness of the room (unlike the clinics she had frequented in the past).

Then a sound arOSe:

...the nurse, standing by the *door* that lead to the examination corridor, said her name:

"Ms. Shoshoni".

Jana did not respond.

"Ms. Shoshoni", the nurse repeated it again.

Jana's mind was somewhere else and she didn't hear her name.

And, maybe she wasn't used to hearing her last name said in an unknown place? [Does that ever happen to you friend?]

The nurse decided to say her full name *slowly* and *loudly* in hopes that one of the *seven* females there would respond:

"Miss"...she paused slightly:

"Jana Helena Mícheál Ó Coileáin Shoshoni"

Jana immediately looked up!

The nurse vocalist stood at the door with a clipboard in her hand.

Jana stood and the vocalist continued: "This way please."

Jana was lead to a back room with a view of a building just opposite the one she was in. She sat down where the nurse directed her to sit.

"I'll be right back dear."

Jana nodded.

Jana sat their thinking about **the-night-before**.

Why did she collapse?

Why did she vomit?

Jana thought **HARD AND LONG** until she figured it out.

"I'm pregnant! Oh shit, I'm pregnant!"

It had just dawn on her that she did not have her period for over a month now.

Usually she would get cramps in her thighs a week before she would have her bloody period.

Jana had gotten NO CRAMPS and NO BLOOD-BLOOD-BLOOD.

The nurse came in and took her vitals.

Jana's weight had increased by seven pounds! (Although her body did not show it).

Jana did not say a word.

She kept quiet.

Jana wanted to confirm with the doctor.

After a while Doctor Ramirez came in.

"Hello I'm Doctor Ramirez": he extended his hand to her.

She obliged and shook his hand.

(a *strange* custom she thought)

$$S = -(n_\mathrm{S} - n_{\overline{\mathrm{S}}})$$

The doctor continued speaking before Jana could reply:

"Miguel told me what happened and it seemed a bit unusual for something just to happen," the doctor said.

"If I were guessing, I say you are pregnant."

'What?" Jana rose her voice.

[How can you **rose a voice!** hmmm.]

"When was your last period?"

Jana sat their thinking (double checking in her mind to make sure of her suspicion.):

"About a month and a half ago."

Dr. Ramirez buzzed the nurse from within the room.

The Vocalist Nurse entered:

VN

"Abigail, can you please bring a pregnancy package: the urinal one."

"Yes doctor... right away."

After the test results Dr. Ramirez told Jana she was two months pregnant.

"Congratulations!"

 The doctor was very professional. He was about Miguel's age of 40.

"I will take a blood test to confirm your exact pregnancy commencement."

"This test will measure the hormone 'human chorionic gonadotropin (hCG)' in your blood:"

"It is called a 'Quantitative hCG Blood Test'".

"Since you did collapse, I will also take other blood tests including one to check your hemoglobin count to make sure you don't have anemia."

The doctor continued:

"If you do I will recommend iron tablets and other appropriate supplements."

"Be aware that your collapse may have been due to not having enough oxygen in your blood."

Dr. Ramirez continued:

"Blood deficiency is common among pregnant women: since the blood volume increases but at a rate that makes some of the essential ingredients in it insufficient."

Jana made a **long** face.

long l o n g face!

"Don't worry dear. It is good that you came in."

"I will also write you a list of recommended maternity doctors from which you can choose."

 Jana gratefully thanked him.

Jana really felt comfortable with this doctor. Doctor Ramirez really seemed to care and know what he was talking about.

In fact Jana thought of him as highly competent compared to all the clinic doctors she **had had** in the past.

[had had]

As Jana drove out of the parking structure, she decided to go to her apartment.

Jana needed to

thin*k* thin*k* thin*k*.

She was worried that Miguel might be upset because of her pregnancy.

In her mind she thought the worst!

Jana's mind was traveling fast and she could not keep to one thought.

Jana began to realize that she was freaking out.

Freak•in Freak•in Freak•in

[and not in the comical sense:( ]

Jana **TENSED** up to an unpleasant state....

```
TENSED
UP! UP! UP!
```

She felt...

... loss † *L*oss ✝ loss †

Jana felt *vulnerable*.

Sh e. Sh e. Sh e.

As Jana began her *flight* up the stairs to her apartment, the neighbor next door noticed her.

"Hi Jana, long time no see! How are you?"

It was Paul from downstairs.

Paul shared one of the apartments in the building with his wife Willa and son Jake.

['Paul Willa Jake'...odd names...especially together!]

"Hi Paul, I'm doing just fine. Thanks for asking. How's your family?"

Paul began to ramble and ramble to the point that Jana was not listening---she could not listen to him. She could not listen to anyone!

any. one.

Jana was incomprehensible in understanding her thoughts and she was about to
EXPLODE!

She was all mixed-up!

Her anx-i-ety became unbearable that she had to interrupt Paul:

"Well Paul, sorry to run, but have a great holiday season."

With that said she smiled a fake smile and began her ascent.

Paul stood staring at her as Jana climbed the stairs.

Jana could feel him looking at her.

Jana increased her speed and immediately opened the door.

As Jana walked in she noticed the absence of her cat.

Jana really began to feel nervous.

She raced through the house and called out the cat's name.

"Wait Jana!", she said to herself...

"He's at the beach house".

Jana stood there as if in limbo.

Some sort of waiting.

...some sort!

Jana didn't even know what she was waiting for!

Maybe she was trying to catch a fleeting thought?

Jana paused her incoherent pacing of blankness and took a deep breath.

Jana realized...

She realized...

Jana realized at that moment...

...that she was now *completely* alone.

The sun had not yet set and the beams of light came in to her living room: hitting her in the face.

Jana so desperately wanted to know what to do:

...she began to pace back and forth in her living room not realizing that she still held her purse in her hand.

Somehow Jana thought she held a *brush*.

She took that imaginary brush to her head to stroke it but instead was hit with the weight of her purse.

"Shit!" she said out loud.

Jana angrily twirled the purse and tossed it across the room.

It hit the wall and fell *straight down*.

Her hairs were raised by the throwing motion and then came down to her face...

Jana didn't care anymore about her appearance.

"*What*?! *What*?!" She yelled to the air.

"*What!?*"

Jana fell to her knees and banged on the floor with her `closed` fists.

[can you have 'closed or open fists?'. In your imagination you can! ...or some sort of fist type! **ipe!**]

Jana began to cry.

What started out like just intermittent tears falling to the ground became...

...rivers of tears...

Jana began to sob loudly.

It became uncontrollable and she sobbed for well over half an hour.

After a while Jana laid herself down onto the floor and lost consciousness in a *pool of sorrow*s.

Jana slept.

The coldness of the wooden floors woke her.

Jana did not know what time it was; time had elapsed and darkness **GRIPPED** the walls.

GRIPPED THE WALLS

The `construct-of-time` had lost its programming:

for Jana.

The new mother went up on her knees and took a deep breath:

...the cold reality was put back-into-place.

`t  i  m  e` began to move again.

Jana stood there on her knees, exhausted by the breaks of reason in her mind.

What was happening to her?

Jana decided not to think of, or to entertain, or to ponder her *irrationalities* at any level for that moment.

How can anyone reason irrational thoughts?

Jana could not reason out the irrational.

[How can you 'reason' the 'irrational' the writer asks you friend?]

[pause]

[pause]

[pause]

[Hmmm.....:by breaking apart the components that constructed the irrational.]

[...bits of rational components that together create what seems irrational what appears irrational...]

[...nothing in all existence (or before it) is irrational! Everything serves a purpose. Everything is by design.]

Did Jana dream?

She did not remember a thing of a dream if she
had any.

Nothing at her apartment existed in an opportune
'space' that could have INTERRUPTED her loss
of consciousness.

Since Jana had moved out she had placed her
home phone in *mute* so that no *rings* rung.

rings rung

rings rung

rings rung

no nada.

N A D A

Jana had arranged this silence. She wanted to
relieve herself of all commitments while at the
apartment....in order to think, to contemplate, to
pull herself together, or to avoid a freak out

(something that nevertheless came irregardless AT her current arrival to an *ancient place)*.

a   n   c   i   e   n   t   p   l   a   c   e

For 5.2 seconds, Jana lightly pressed her entire hands against her face to attempt to relieve tension...seeking consolation, rest, to forget.

Jana was at rest at this point.

The tension had been gone for quite some time, Jana was just going through the motions of habit.

Her face felt like fragile *Gelo*. A seven year debatical had come to an end.

What!?

The tantalizing deceits of her negative mind had exhausted Jana to the point where she felt she had pushed them out of her!

Those annoying spirits programmed to seek and *destroy* had been kicked out!

In fact, Jana began to feel better as she awoke to the coldness of the floor.

Jana felt calm and her body was completely at ease.

Jana reached for the ground to push herself to stand on two feet and then proceeded to sit on her tiny sofa.

Jana began to think: but *now* with an open mind.

Open Mind

a free mind!

"Okay", she thought, "Well, I am pregnant."

"Pregnant!"

Jana became excited.

She had always wanted a child and almost never felt it was the right time.

At first Jana resisted such an idea and then she wanted to have a child; but then her partner at the time did not think it was the right time!

But now she had *no choice*.

"I'm pregnant!"

But the *no choice* was a blessing!

The thought to care and love **an innocent** coming into this world just thrilled Jana.

No choice became a *euphoria*, a want, a longing, a desire, **an inspiration**.

Jana wanted to be a mother!

Jana wanted that desire deep-down-inside **every woman**:

...to nurture a glimpse of innocence in the eyes of a child that resembles oneself.; to be able to positively contribute in molding another human being into an independent being.

Some see this as a way to behave like a "*god*" or a "*goddess*": placing one's authority into the fate of a captured spirit!

Not Jana not this woman.

N O T   N O T   N O T

For Jana it was an opportunity to love a being that reflected both her and the man she loved: Miguel.

Jana sat there fully recharging into a perspective frame-of-mind that brought her *firmly* back to

peace peace peace.

After looking at images created by her mind from *crevices* on the ceiling: Jana became aware that she needed to take control of her life; to let her destiny or destinies work themselves out.

Jana realized that there are some things she can control and other things she must leave to fate.

And to fate she was beginning to surrender.

NOT an unknown surrender: but rather Hope and Faith knowing that at the end everything will be as it will be:

A conclusion that has no beginning and no end; a conclusion that has no positive, no negative but *an is* ...something formless and eternal.......

A conclusion of *origin*.

Jana had hoped Miguel would be thrilled.

But now, having had an *open window* to a truth, Jana felt secure in herself and in her inspiration; knowing that no matter what: she was going to be a mother.

a mother!!!

Jana picked up her cell phone to check her messages:

none!

No missed calls either!

Why had Miguel not called or texted her? It was already close to midnight!

"Miguel would be home by now and wondering where I am; especially since I didn't leave a note or a text or message."

 Jana decided not to jump to conclusions.

Jana decided she needed to sleep in her own bed tonight and just relax and *build* an image of how she wanted things to be.

build an image ...

...of how...she wanted... things...

... to be.

[or not to be, that is the question:) Guillermo Shakespeare!:) a.k.a. Guillermo Sanchez of Spanish decent!']

Since grade school Jana would create realities that were predictable to her. In this way, she would not jump to any conclusions or freak out with unexpected news.

However this tactic or technique obviously wasn't full-proof in a world that was constantly changing.

constantly   changing

And her receiving critical news she did not phantom creating realities for: like the surprise news of her pregnancy: was **definitely**

tactic intolerant! tactic immune! tactic resistant!

Jana went to her bedroom and began to slowly undress herself.

Jana stood in front of her mirror (a new mirror she bought to replace the one that had broken after her lapse into unconsciousness from times past).

There she stood...looking at herself.

Jana could not see visual signs of her pregnancy.

Jana caressed her tummy and began to talk to her unborn child—reassuring it that she loved it; not quite human yet; at least not an-oxygen-breathing-one-that-uses-lungs.

The sex of her child did not matter to her---she would love it the same regardless.

The child was in transition of being transported, even if only in part, to a world Jana was not completely sure of: something did not fit well in her mind as to her environment.

Jana stood their contemplating about the world (her environment).

"How could it be that no one on this planet knows their true origin?" she asked herself in her mind.

Deep down inside Jana knew that those in power (all governments, all so-called religious leaders and organizations, the large corporate elite conglomerates, and others at the top serving these upper social strata) knew the true reason why we are here in this environment (the true reasons away from the created-and-masking religious reasons placed to distract us from the truth!).

"yet"....Jana thought...

"...They hold the truth from the masses because something would not ultimately benefit the masses: something harmful".

Jana further concluded **just then**:

"It's like taking an animal to slaughter: the taker doesn't tell the animal (to be slaughtered) where it is going or where it resides."

"This non-disclosure or hints at the truth is kept from the animal so that the animal goes quietly without any resistance! It goes blindly (naively) to its doom!"

"The human being ..."

"...and other beings:" she continued analyzing this topic...

"Energies encased *into* organic material:"

" Carbon".

"By choice or imprisonment?"

That uncertainty of her environment and their possible implications **bothered** Jana.

Like most humans, Jana thought *infrequently* about such topics...maybe to pretend they didn't exist; maybe to say 'well I can't do anything about it anyway so why bother thinking about what I can't change?'.

At that moment Jana decided to clear her mind of her suspicions and to stop delving more into the "environment" topic.

Jana decided then to pretend something is not going on...no hidden agendas by those in power.

Jana decided instead to seek solace in ignorance (even if it truly was just 'pretend' ignorance).

[Besides, if we knew a bit of the truth: many of us would anyway regress REGRESS and go back into being **dIsTracTeD** from the truth...this distraction is the goal of those that rule the world.]

[And in truth: the whole system, including the **filter**, the **human brain**, (not our *eternal mind*), **serves as a BIG** distraction.]

[Other distractions include livelihood priority, survival priority, hormonal impositions, and mind programming: the Medias of Communication (print, music, news, motion pictures, television programs, e-d-u-c-a-t-i-o-n), sports, imposed

ambitions *imposed ambitions* IMPOSED
AMBITIONS, and the list goes on and on.]`

[Maybe Jana wasn't ready to let go of this world
and its deceits?: who could since the immersion is
so **PENETRATING**!]

[P E N E** T R A ** T I N G**]

[The distraction of Cultures created: their customs,
religious limitations, narrow-and-suffocating
views, imposed-freedoms, their condemnations,
and so on and so on and so on are so entrenched in
our minds.]

[is **ignorance** bliss? No. It is
DANGEROUS!]

[d   a   n   JUR
     o   u   s !]

Jana began to see the reflection of her face: a face
that had gone through its share of experiences.

In this reflection Jana saw that she was still alive
to be different than she had ever been.

ever bin

As Jana stood their breathing deeply, as in a mantra, she remembered the vision of the night before.

Jana wanted SO MUCH to go back to that vision! Jana felt empowered and protected by the family tribe in her vision.

Jana wanted to feel that same purpose of her vision in her life now---and this new child within her offered that; it offered a responsibility which was now hers.

Jana pulled the drapes of the shower and went in her tub and turned-on the water. It ran cold for a while and then warm. The sting of temperature changes reminded her of **this life**.

Jana then opened the man-made shower head sphincter. MAN-MADE. The water felt warm: like rivers of waters *cleansing* her body.

Jana stood their partially receiving her baptism into a new life: a life that would change her *forever*.

Jana then lowered her head to receive the full baptism of the waters.

Jana now became one with her reality---a reality she had **not created** but which she embraced now: *completely*.

After taking in the waters, Jana decided that it was time for bed: she wanted to start her day right and go for a walk in the morning (for now she could not run. She thought: "I have to be careful with my body!").

Jana decided not to call Miguel.

She wanted this night to be hers.

Jana would only answer the phone if Miguel called.

MíGüel

After drying herself completely, Jana headed straight to bed: naked.

BEING *NAKED* made her feel freer... no constraints... just a lessening of one's coverings...a freedom not to judge or to be judge... just an *is*.

On her way to her bed Jana warmed up the apartment: setting the thermostat to 70-

7.

As she entered her bed the sheets were cold.

Jana lay there speaking to her child and told it that everything was going to be okay, and that she was looking forward to meeting her or him when it was time.

Jana told the child about her happy moments as a child; the beautiful moments, the rare moments Jana spent with her mother and her father at the same time.

As Jana continued to SPEAK *S-L-E-E-P* overtook her and she stopped.

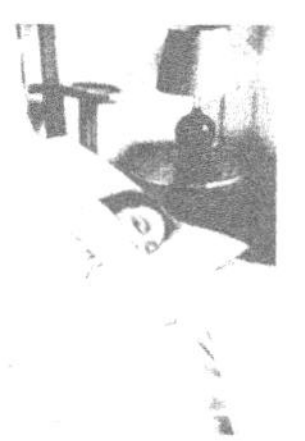

Chapter SEVENteen
A *New* Resolution

Miguel slept well that night with no worries. He had received a call from Dr. Ramirez informing him of Jana's pregnancy, and congratulating him on becoming a new father to be!

Miguel knew Jana needed time and trusted her to make the right decision.

Miguel loved Jana more than anyone he had ever loved.

He loved her quirky way of being at times and her seriousness at other times.

And, he loved to help her as much a possible feel secure when she became insecure and emotional.

Jana brought *life* into Miguel's life.

A life that was filled with growth—Miguel felt his personal growth increase just being around Jana. She had this vibrant energy to her he could not explain.

Yup! She was special and he knew it:)

Miguel also knew Jana was on that journey to fulfillment. And that *inspired* him.

Jana was a being he had contemplated meeting when he was a child: someone who would give him Hope and Faith and peace just being with that person.

And here she was! He had met her at a **café KKanaKoluKKūMāhā**!

In the past, Miguel had depended on himself to make important decisions; to find ways to grow positively in his inner workings.

Unbalanced though he was: apart from his successful business decisions, Miguel had limited growth in his self-inner workings. Miguel knew that **true exponential personal growth** comes with solemn relationships.

---relationships that take time to mature into **illuminating existences**.

Illuminating existences that, when secured in knowledge, Faith, Hope, love, and a good fear of God (respect), bring forth contentment, everlasting peace, patience, eternal joy, and by default: viably profound solutions to any life challenges and to the beyond!

And Jana was that catalyst for change *In-His-Life* to begin to bring forth an **illuminating existence** beyond the physical.

And as to personal relationships between 2 loving intimate partners, Miguel was convinced that a *relationship of true intimate friendship* goes both ways where one receives help as well as give it: in all areas imaginable...including in the area of emotions and unresolved issues.

Miguel's decision to refrain from calling or texting Jana was firm. It was, however, difficult to refrain since they had frequently exchanged communication in these ways during the day, or while he was away on business.

Miguel remembered her last text three days ago:

Querido,

Don't eat a heavy lunch. I am preparing something special for you.

Algo auténtico.

La Mujer que te ama,

Jana

That was a beautiful night as all nights were:
There were no fights or major disagreements.
Each partner in this intimate relationship showed
affection in many ways.

That night Jana had cooked a Mexican dish from
scratch. Jana made the most beautiful chicken
enchiladas! And she made the sauce from scratch!
She bought all fresh ingredients; nothing from
cans or any type of processed food!

And the salad and wine to accompany the dish just
made everything even more pleasant.

On that night, when Miguel came from the office,
he found the home with dimmed lights; she used
only candle lights!

This made him feel so so special that Jana would take the time to get the recipe and prepare something with such love.

such love

Honestly, Miguel felt kind of awkward at first since he had never had any woman he dated take the time to make something so so special.

When Miguel arrived to this *special place*, Jana greeted him at the door and asked him to close his eyes. She led him with her hand to the dining room table. Jana had moved it to the center of the living room just for this occasion.

Heavy! How did she move it?!!!

Miguel sat with his eyes closed.

"Keep them close Querido!"

Jana hurried to the kitchen and returned with the dish. Oh something smelled so so ¡delicioso!

"Open" she said.

The food was marvelous and half way through Jana leaned over and kissed Miguel: they kissed for quite a while and then Jana pulled back and said, "Eat your food Querido! Más tarde

tendremos más de ése
postre!:)"

That night was *m e m o r a b le*.

Jana insisted on serving him like a king! When Miguel wanted to help remove the dishes, she stopped him.

Afterwards Jana led Miguel to the bedroom and unclothed him while caressing *every*-part-of-him.

It turned out to be such a beautiful and lasting night that Miguel woke up at 10 a.m. the following day!

Back to the present, Miguel closed his eyes and slept well.

In his dreams he reminisced all the beautiful moments he had spent with Jana to this point in time.

Miguel was content in his heart. And in all confidence, Miguel saw Jana *be* who Jana *Is* and who Jana *is* to become!

The next morning was Wednesday, November 28, 2007. Jana woke at 9 a.m., made the bed, got dressed and headed out of the apartment.

When Jana arrived at Miguel's, she noticed that his car was not in the garage.

Jana parked her car and headed to the boardwalk to begin her new-routine-of-walking. She had decided on walking at least 34 minutes each day.

Jana headed south toward the Santa Monica Pier.

As Jana walked she received many smiles from all kinds of people that passed her by. Jana felt as if they knew of her pregnancy and were congratulating her on her new mission on becoming a mother.

Jana smiled back and continued walking.

All the while, she thought of seeing Miguel tonight. Jana did not want to call or text him. She wanted to meet him and give him the news personally.

Jana's mind wondered to her vision on the day she fell ill. She felt so alive in that dream and the desire to return to it had N-O-T receded.

n   o   t   r   e   c   e   d
                    e   d

It was locked up in a corner of her *eternal mind* that eagerly sought a return.

r   e   t   u   r
                      n

Jana felt that **SOME** entity was giving her a message through this vision.

Just then Jana remembered her father.

"What happened to daddy?", she whispered out loud.

"Where are you daddy?".

Jana began to feel a deep feeling of depression---a sadness that began growing around her---

"Stop, stop Jana!" Jana yelled aloud at herself.

The people around became STARTLED and STARED at her.

Jana kept walking.

Jana needed to control that feeling that many times before in her past brought her to a

plight-of-darkness

...where she would spend endless days in her closet *wishing* to die.

STERBEN Morir chê't

BMNPA TN

But *every time*, during those bleak days, Jana would find encouragement out-of-nowhere to continue her life.

Back then Jana thought about seeing a doctor concerning these bouts-of-depression. Every time though she decided to fight it herself.

Back then Jana didn't want to take medication or share her deepest thoughts with others.

Because of unresolved issues in her **human mind** to the present, Jana thought (at that moment in her walking) that maybe it **be-best** she *write* something to express these unresolved issues.

Or, to use *writing* as a method to explore a path to an unknown that would direct her to something beyond her limited **egg-shell** mind.

Trying to resolve unnatural issues using a **limited-capacity-processor** (naturally tainted with manipulators and inconsistors by design) (that is: the **human mind**) was limiting.

A better processor for Jana was to explore issues with her ***eternal*** mind (which she was unaware of possessing). A mind without the filter: the human brain.

Like most humans, we don't differentiate or tend to differentiate between a mind processing thought through a filter (the brain) and mind processing thought through an eternal structure housing the true unadulterated mind.

...an ***eternal mind*** which POSSESSES all the answers!

ALL THE ANSWERS

Irrespective of knowing these differences in her present, Jana decided on *writing* as a form of therapy!

therapy

 Knowing now that she was going to be a mother, Jana did not want to have these HANG-UPS---J

Her desire was to be an excellent mother.

As her day's selected walk-path reached Ocean Park Blvd on the beach boardwalk, Jana turned around to complete her walk ending at the beach house.

Her enthusiasm began to grow within her as she thought about writing...and in particular she was thinking of writing *a novel.*

[*A novel...*deliberately set as fiction when in reality it is not fiction at all.]

[...rather *a novel* is a manifested reality dispersing true experiences and thoughts that have been lived somewhere *in*-*and*-*beyond* the fabric of time.]

After a while on thinking on this subject of writing, Jana broke her spell-of-thought and picked up her pace and walked at a brisk count.

Coming into her physical present location, Jana began to observe the people around her.

Jana began to smile every time she passed someone: greeting them positively. [psycho!]

Simultaneously, Jana began to focus on her breathing and on the air that came into her lungs.

Jana slowly exhaled at intervals to help her focus on nothing.

This breathing gave her inner tranquility.

Jana then imaged the small life *within* her; "I love you dear" she said to it and continued her mantra.

When Jana got home she changed clothes and went to the kitchen.

Wanting to be a good mother and lover, Jana prepared the necessary ingredients for dinner.

It was only about noon, but she wanted to have everything ready for the final combining-and-cooking of-the-ingredients at around 5 p.m....

...cutting the amount of time of cooking dinner near the serving time of about 6 or 7.

Jana finished the preparations at 1:30 p.m.

She placed everything in containers and after they cooled, she placed them in the refrigerator.

Jana really wanted to make sure Miguel would not eat something after work so she decided to text him.

Jana reached for her phone and then observed:

No calls or texts received!

Jana wrote her text to Miguel:

Querido y Vida Bella,

I have something special to share with you tonight.

Please try to be here by 6:30 p.m.

I am preparing dinner.

I love you and I will explain why I could not come home last night.

La mujer que te ama,

JS

Jana wanted to write more. She wanted to let him know now! NOW!

But, Jana withheld from doing so.

"It would be best if I waited".

She sent the message and placed the phone down.

Jana took a quick rinse in the shower, dressed, then grabbed her keys and headed out.

Jana wanted to find out about her Native American past. She had an inkling-of-an-idea that she wanted to write something about her ancestral roots on her father's side.

Jana decided to go to the main branch of the Santa Monica Public Library on 7th and Santa Monica Boulevard.

Jana parked on the street meters and went in looking for a librarian to help her.

"Excuse me mam", she directed her attention toward a librarian there: an Anglo Saxon woman in her late twenties with yellow-orange hair and freckles.

"I want to know about Native Americans in and near Oklahoma."

"I'm not the librarian, sorry", said the woman sitting on a desk marked "Librarian".

"Let me get someone to help you."

The woman hurried off and returned.

"Ms. Donaldson will be here shortly to help you."

As Jana waited, she continued to contemplate possible topics for her novel; Jana began narrowing down her ideas based on inspiration.

I N S P I R A T I O N

Jana then thought of her father: "Maybe I'll write about my father and make up his past which I really don't know anything about".

"Maybe I'll focus on his childhood: describing him growing up in a broken past where life on a reservation was difficult after the numerous conquests, at all levels of repetitive defeat and removal, by the English and Spanish, and now the European Americans."

Too many "maybes".

Jana was scrambling.

^7>!\`/,<-_^\7>!\`/,<-_^\   ...

Verschlüsselung .

The process-of-direction seemed to be a challenging-work-in-progress!

Formulating an idea with a reduced topic of inspiration became verschwommen.

Although brumoso, Jana had narrowed it down to a Native American *male child.*

The idea became narrower: "something of *a being* it seems who was stripped from his roots and left to die".

Jana wanted to be a voice for those uprooted, those forgotten, those dismembered from their self-concept of SELF:

....beings **GENOCIDED** by the AngloWestern Expansion of Greed and Corruption in the Americas.

... from one corner of the continent to the other.

Jana's heart began to *PALPITATE* faster as she thought the *meanings* and *implications* of these "RAPE" words.........

Anger began to build up inside her:
an *Unquenchable Fire* to Destroy the wills of the Anglo-European Anglo American "**STRIPPERS**"!

Sie **née-ded** to calm herself down.

Unconsciously Jana thought:

"The redress of such matters is already in motion."

[not really]

Jana decided to veer her mind-energies toward a topic of focus of a child-being *from a time* before the completion of the Conquests of the Americas.

Jana didn't want her writing to come from *anger*: a catalyst reserved for more productive processes already in motion to end the Rebellion that are the UNIVERSES, the *scattered matter*, te mea hanga.

Jana Not being fully aware of underlining realities... due to her evaporating human encasement, never-the-less `unconsciously` concluded that she would play a part in ending the "energy wars" found in the Universes in order to End the UNIVERSES!

ENERGY WARS

Or, as those humans on the very top, the cusps of societies, of all world cultures, know but conceal to the masses call it:

"STAR WARS"

Back to the present, Jana stood there in front of the empty "Librarian" chair.

She stood there in front of the vibrating energies within the matter.

Jana stood there in front of her thoughts.

"A little research in the library will probably direct me toward an exact-condensed-topic to write about. I'll keep an open-mind and decide once I start."

As one thought entered Jana....one thought was shelved.

Order began to take place in Jana's mind.

 "Hello, can I help you?" a short black woman asked Jana as she approached.

Jana was consolidating-her-thoughts and could not answer the woman until she completed her thought-process as to the developing novel in her mind.

"Hello!" the woman **raised** her voice.

Jana just `stared` in-her-mind using whatever `view` was-in-front of her as a `screen` to-*write*-on...

(a screen she, and the metaphysicals, and the UNADULTERATED-CARBONLESS could `only` see).

The librarian, **a bit** startled, kind of **understood** Jana (being a pencil-neck herself!).

"Well, I'll be right here if you need my assistance," the short black woman said and went behind the information desk console marked "Librarian".

Yes, Jana thought, Yes!

Jana directed her attention to the librarian. "I'm sorry. No, I don't need your help right now. Sorry for the interruption".

Jana headed toward the exit and to her car.

What excited her was that she did not want to start off her novel referencing Native American historical or cultural facts. No, she did not want to do that!

Not do that That Not do!

Not do!

Instead, Jana just wanted to focus *first* on a child's point of view experience in a desolate place where encouraement was gained and lost and gained again: where people waited.

Waited!

Jana would use the information she already had about child development to carve out her reality of a mind of a child....and in particular this Native-American male child.

Unconsciously Jana was hoping that the genetics of her Comanche side could help tailor this knowledge to her story.

What craziness is this?!!!

[Craziness is often labeling things not completely understood...uncommon things...and uncommon due to the restrictions and perceptions imposed on the masses by the INSTALLED dominate cultures.]

[sad but true]

When Jana reached her car she PAUSED.

Jana started to feel *rickety* again about everything---bouts of insecurity wanted to take control of her.

It seemed an onslaught of Ricket-Monsters (RM) wanted to invade her body: twisting it as if she were a newborn entry-unit (Not only tearing and reforming her physical but her *peace* along with it...seeking to replenish its RM's thirst through her inspiration).

Soranus had identified it simply as physical, but it seems it was much more than that!: a programmed destroyer set to dismantle the energy within to

such an extreme that it made it easy for the objective to digest its purloined nourishment.

Jana remained *paused* in her motions:

Standing there CLAS*PING* the *points-of-time* at its corners! Jana would not let go of her firm *GRA*SP on it; As-if frenziedly complaining to it..... and forcing-it to change her ***fortuities*** to a *flowery serendipity.*

A-past-and-common-bout of **FETISH** behavior wanted to engulf her to the point of rocking her off her Hor-se (the **R**aging **A**nimal).

It seemed that these increased feelings were related to her body's changing-hormonal-composition related to her pregnancy.

But the anno$_{13}$yance continued!

Phreneticus   **P**hreneticus   **P**hreneticus

...the demon-child relentless in its collaboration with the *whole-scheme* of military coups.

But Not This Time!!!...

Jana fought it by positively saying—I'm doing the right thing. I will change but it will be gradual. I will change but on my time. Jana said this *mantra* as she went into her car and started it.

Jana kept the repetition as she d-*rove* home.

By the time Jana was at Miguel's: she felt better.

She had won the battle.

Jana did not realize the reasons for her insecurities but knew that she was not alone with her issue:

Jana knew everyone fought some **DEMON** that sought to disrupt peace within the being.

Jana reassured herself that it would be different for her and that somehow (maybe through her writing) she would help people.

Jana knew that she needed to do more to serve people—She needed to-get-out-of-herself [a difficult task for all humans when everything around spells: Me, Myself, and I-ris.] [Geoffrey's and his counterparts' contributions served no true enlightenment toward the freedom Jana and all EEBs aramak...... جستجو وکردن..... tìm kiếm].

When Jana stepped into her peace-home: she undressed on the spot:

....feeling the elements brush on her nerves.....soothing them to a-stillness from *a-storm-of-strikes*!

Jana sat in a crisscross-apple-sauce position right in the hall way.

She breathed profoundly and took in the coldness that crept from the floor.

Not*-a-*T*-*hought entered her that rustled any sort of uneasiness.

Bool•e•an Free!

After a restful while she walked into the hall-bathroom and began to urinate.

Jana then headed to the showers for a longer session: She cleansed-herself in a warm-shower-of-love.

Immediately thereafter [yes THEREAFTER] she headed to the bedroom.

As Jana walked she picked up her *fallen* clothes.

Jana decided to put on shorts and a blouse. She wanted to look *plain* for Miguel; she wanted him to look at her in "a plain perspective": wearing simple clothes that did not have anything to do with style or a current fashion.

Jana wore NO make-up.

THEREAFTER Jana proceeded to the kitchen and brought out all the alimentary items for the night's dinner and finished preparing them.

Jana made:

- chicken breast marinated in soy sauce (yea!:)
- broccoli with cauliflower in light butter (hooray!)
- and CREAMY mashed potatoes (oh my J!:)

Once prepared, all Jana needed to do now was to warm them and combine them on a plate when the time-of-consumption neared.

Jana thought for a moment..."hummm?".

"Yes, let's a a a a-*dda:*"

"Garlic bread" [a bit *PI·*QUANT don't you think Jana?]

Jana then headed to the cellar downstairs and got a *clear* champagne.

Jana knew nothing about particular champagne brands....but she had some competence in this area to make sure it was a clear yellow. [okay Jana now you're overdoing it!:'J]

While warming and setting up the food in a neat fashion, Jana thought about the endless days of being ALONE most of the time in her apartment...

cooking for herself. Her only guests then were herself, her cat!, and her aquarium fishes.

Even as a child living with her mother, Jana would cook for both of them...ALONE.

Jana's mother worked the "graveyard shift", so when she arrived Jana would be asleep. Her mother would go to the kitchen and see a specialty prepared plate of food made by Jana.

Jana thought of her mother.

"Mama would eat it, drink some wine, and go to sleep". Jana spoke to herself in her mind.

In that situation, Jana would wake up early to go to school. After preparing her mother's food and dressing herself, she headed out by 6:11 a.m. toward the bus stop...a routine that became mechanical for her...some sort of ritual she felt.

Jana didn't have those quality-moments-of-mother-being-home and helping her prepare for her day at school. Jana was ALONE even-back-then.

In fact, in these industrialized nations, such a setting of being ALONE is common place for many children with middle to lower incomes households.

"Latch-Key" kids they call us...US...being alone and not having proper guidance. Many children get into trouble or seek attention by means that are counter-productive...some seek drugs, prostitution, boyfriends and girlfriends early on, violence, gang affiliations for attention, and some wake to criminal activities as a pass-time or as a way of making money to feed themselves and to gather enough money to pay the household rent!

rent!

[thievery allowed by the government!]

Another sector of these-type-of-children find other ways of coping with their respective-lack-of-proper attention: some become **LONERS** throughout their life, or others become too caring individuals that allow others to take advantage of them throughout their adolescent and adult lives, or others develop sleeping disorders like Jana.

It appears that Jana's mother had a choice as to "graveyard shift". Her mother nevertheless chose this "shift" for reasons not-clear-to-Jana.

Jana's memory of her mom: never loving in a sense of showing **MUCH** emotion.

MUCH affection.

MUCH of anything.

Doris, Jana's mother, would hug her daughter: but *that action* felt mechanical and not really **genuine.**

not **genuine**

No. not **genuine.**

Jana's mother always seemed to have something in her mind.. running...

RUNNING...

...something that would not let her be...

...in peace.

When Jana finished the food for her and Miguel the-clock-marked 5:38 p.m.

Jana covered the food and began to set the small table in the kitchen for dinner.

Jana could have set the large dining room table, but she wanted to make everything as `plain` as possible.

Ironically, Jana wasn't even sure why she wanted to keep it `plain`!

 `plain.`

"Maybe", she thought, "I want it `plain` so that the surroundings and the food being served looked as regular as possible so that the breaking of the pregnancy news would stand out and shine to Miguel!?"

Jana was *pensive*.

Jana started to conclude that she wanted it down-to-Earth so that Miguel would not draw any illusions in his mind of grandeur-of-prospect that things would be easy in having and caring for a child.

"Shit!"

...this began not to make any sense to Jana.

Jana stopped thinking and finished setting the table.

Exactly at 5:56 p.m., the door began to open from the garage.

Miguel was home! :)

Hooooray!:)

Jana's pulse increased with a mixture of excitement and doubt: but it was more excitement since she wanted this.

She wanted this.

Jana sat herself at the table, calming herself down, and waited to see Miguel.

The pulse elevations seemed to be on a frequency-of-intermittency.

The *revolving-door* seemed to open and close on Jana.

As Miguel walked to the kitchen he was all smiles!

In his hand he held a bouquet-of-*white*-roses, and the smile that accompanied it (gleaming from his face) was incomparable!

incomprehensible!

Jana had never seen *that* smile!

She smiled back.

Miguel slightly knelt before Jana and kissed her gently and slowly.

He ***breathed-her-in*** (and she took the opportunity to do likewise).

Miguel delicately handed Jana the flowers saying:

"For a beauty ***bey***ond compare."

Miguel knelt down before her and continued:

"A jewel of the *Nile!*"

Miguel slowly and elegantly waved his hand upward and said:

"To the *Pearl* of *Judea*!"

Jana blushed.

After a *moment's* pause, Miguel went to the kitchen and reached for a glass vase in one of the cabinets, filled it with water, and placed it on the center of the table.

Jana was about to place the beautiful white flowers inside the vase, when Miguel eloquently stopped her saying:

"Relax Sweet Heart." He offered his hands to her and Jana placed the bouquet of beauty into his hands.

After another *moment's* pause, Jana then was about to get up to bring the food and Miguel again stopped her saying:

"Please, let me do it My Love".

Jana was about to insist, but Miguel stood and headed to the kitchen's marbled counter and brought the plates covered in plastic and placed them on the table.

Miguel took the covers off and smiled.

"Wow, smells great! I'll be back in a moment."

Miguel turned around and Jana said,

"Honey, the champagne is in the refrigerator!"

Miguel raced to the refrigerator and pulled out a bottle, popped it open and headed toward the table.

The champagne glasses sat *waiting.*

waiting.

waiting.

Miguel poured *l*iquid *c*rystal into the champagne cups slowly, and then placed the bottle down.

Emotions rang high and the champagne took on a metaphorical form in the interchanges.

intra-*changes* ...appeared

to fluxuate in uncertain directions **for Jana at that moment**.

Internments of Old Ideas began

to be unshelved **for Jana at that moment**.

Interred Ideas Of Past fluxuated in

chaos **for Jana at that moment**.

Yet Jana defeated the negativities in her mind with positive reinforcements for a better now and a better future.

Jana was beginning to gain control over her emotions in shorter intervals...declaring her independence to all long standing negativities that in the past had invaded her mind for long intervals of time.

As the *l*iquid *c*rystal began to settle inside the glasses, Miguel said gently:

"Ahorita vengo amor"

Miguel walked toward the garage and after a minute and a second, brought back a large box wrapped in colorful, flowery white paper.

Miguel carefully placed the large gift on the floor between his chair and hers.

Jana looked at it in surprise.

Her optimism began growing by exponential proportions!

Jana said nothing.

Miguel carefully sat down.

After another *moment's* pause of sitting quietly, they both began to eat...

...as if they read each other's mind...like members of an orchestra...ready to start at the keenest-indication-of-commencement-of-a-classical-piece-of-music...even before the conductor raises his (or her) hand!

 Jana kept looking over at the large present.

Jana was about to speak when Miguel intercepted her:

"Sweet heart: have some champagne".

Jana reached for her cup and sipped it and was about to take a *gulp* when she remembered she was now-pregnant and placed the glass down without another touch-of-the-glass-to-her-lips.

"Miguel, I have something to tell you and…"

Miguel again intercepted her future words and said:

"Open the present first."

"But, I need to tell you about…"

 Miguel quickly came over and knelt in front of Jana and kissed her on the lips: impeding any more coherent-sounds-from-Jana.

A *tingle* of hormonal reaction *pinged* Jana and she began to softly kiss Miguel more and more. Jana felt the passion burning inside her and she clasped his head with her hands…increasing the intensity of her kisses.

After the release of the Seventh kiss, at which Jana **somewhat** softly-paused, Miguel said, *momentarily* exhausted:

"Sweet heart, open the present first and then we'll talk."

Miguel stood up, cleared the table, and placed the present on top of it.

Jana stared at it wondering what on earth was inside the large box!

On top of the box there was a small envelope; Jana reached for it and opened it.

A small note inside the envelope read:

> *I am happy for*
> *both of us!*
> *Miguel*

Did he know? Jana thought.

Without allowing anymore conclusions to enter her mind: Jana unwrapped the large plain, white flowery box.

What Jana found inside was another box made of pure white hue paper like a White Rose!...Jana carefully opened it at the corners and reached in and pulled out a white-and-**black** baby car seat!

"Doctor Ramirez told me about your pregnancy. I was about to worry not knowing your whereabouts since you were not home. And, at that moment, I received a call from him."

"He is after all one-of-my-best-friends!:)"

Miguel continued.....

"I am delighted and happy Sweety!"

Miguel knelt again and kissed Jana.

Jana sat there not knowing what to say.

She didn't have to say anything!

Or, reveal.....

any*thing!*

 Jana developed a thought and said:

"So you are happy?"

Tears began to flow down from her eyes' duct glands.

"Is this what you wanted?", Jana asked.

She *tear*-ed some more....

...not knowing what she was feeling but for sure Jana was feeling something deep down inside her.

Miguel pulled up a chair and held her hand with both of his hands as if protecting it:

But Miguel's limb-choreography was not a topic of protection but rather of **deep, eternally** *felt* gesture of:

Love

     Amor

       Yêu

         Sevgi

           Els*ker*

             Pag-Ibig

           Rakkaus

         Zu Lieben

     Maite

   Ame

Láska

Ljubezen

Grá

Aroha

Ki-po-na Aloha

No exact variant of the meaning put into symbols or vocal sounds could properly portray the TRUE JOY Miguel felt inside for Jana and their child.

"I am happy my love because we are having a union of our love: a child."

He continued:

"This child was conceived out of the love I have for you."

"You Jana are the woman of my dreams."

"You Jana are the woman that brings me happiness unlike anyone I have ever known."

"You, my Sweet Heart, are the person I feel most comfortable with in this world of many *unpredictable* events."

Jana blushed: no one had ever declared such a thing about her or had shown such warmth, sincerity, devotion*!*

"How do you feel about it?" Miguel asked Jana.

Still being held Jana declared:

"I am very happy."

"...Very happy!"

Jana nodded harmoniously with her emotions as if ripples coming from the core of her being.

Tears continued to flow from Jana.

Tears of Joy, Tears of Relief, Tears of Contentment.

Jana continued:

"This child means a lot to me."

"It means that I will finally care for a being that will love me unconditionally from the start."

"It is a child that brings many hopes for the future".

"Being **pregnant** gives me that deep-**yearning**-of-wanting-to-be-a-**mother** and care for a new being...a new life!"

"Whether it is a boy or a girl, I will love it the *Sam*e."

"I will do my best to be the best parent I can be."

Jana said this remembering her mother.

Although her mother had not been there for her emotionally: Jana nevertheless unconditionally loved and loves her mother no matter what.

...no matter **what!**

Jana loved and loves her father too.

...but living with her mother Jana felt a need to love her mother more.

Maybe because she spent more time with her; maybe because Jana felt resentment that her father had stopped seeing her.

Franc-ly, Jana did not know exactly how to see her emotions; how to evaluate them since *being* in her emotions clouded her judgments in such matters.

This time, Jana thought, I will try to do it right for my child.

This time Jana was determined that the story would be different; it would be a **better** *life* for this being-inside-her.

That night was extra special: both parents were able to *anticipate* together the *coming* of their child; the coming of a new life (dismissing any references of *death* or *extinctions*).

The Jana Trilogy Novel Continues on Book 2 subtitled:

"*Book* 2 *of 3*

Sun Shone Search for Truth"

· · · · · · ·

<u>Message from Mi'Kha-el Feeza:</u>

Mi'Kha-el Feeza WEBSITE:

Eternoi.Com

Buenos Días Reader!

Regeneration of Love and Resistance for the common good is working at my website. We are looking for like-minded individuals and organizations to collectively help rid ourselves of the ills of our communities in this world peacefully.

We seek to bring the betterment of the common good to the forefront of the consciousness of every single human being, A.I., and extraterrestrial. And in so doing, bring fruitful, constructive change, peacefully, to all of the world's and Earth's inhabitants for the benefit of all as a whole!

If you'd like to join one of our committees for the Regeneration of Love and Resistance…come visit and join!:) The more free minds the better! Together we are a Collective Mind that is bringing change to the world and the Earth for the betterment of the common good! We are Eternoi Humanitarian Organization (Eternoi).

We, Eternoi, believe there is a good fruitful solution to every ill in this world and on this planet! God gave us a mind to

think! Let's use it for the common good! We are wholly
Volunteer Based. We never collect any monies directly into
the organization as a whole. Any expenses to promote an
Eternoi solution to a world ill are paid by each member, as to
each member's own will and ability, directly to the service
provider, vendor, etc. Example of expenses includes assembly
permit fees, etc. Consequently and by design, every member
of Eternoi is a volunteer, including the leadership. We, Eternoi,
never solicit expense monies from anyone OUT OF the
Eternoi membership body. Specific committees are involved
in seeing which members are willing and able to help pay the
Eternoi solution expenses, as described, directly to the service
provider, etc.

And, Eternoi membership is always FREE. One becomes an
Eternoi member after being successfully vetted to a specific
committee. We believe in the goodness of every single human
being. We believe that change for the betterment of the
common good comes by example, encouragement, and by
awareness!

Have Faith and have Hope and move forward in love!

May God the Father, who is in Heaven and within us, bless
you always!

Sincerely,

Mi'Kha-el Feeza
eternoi@protonmail.com

ACKNOWLEDGEMENTS AND NOTES

All final output Images in the novel by the author. All Artwork in the novel by the author. All final versions images found in the novel created by the author. Origins of some raw images used as a base for artwork by the author originating from elsewhere in their raw original format noted below.

Only Raw Free Use Images (from pexels.com, pixaybay.com, et al.) or Raw Pubic Domain images used from their original format into the author's artwork where used in the novel, where final artwork arrangements of images where made by the author. All other images in the novel produced exclusively by the author.

The author would like to thank and acknowledge the following people for their contributions in preparing the novel for publication:

Craig Longshore from the Oklahoma Forestry Services at Sallisaw in 2015, Friday, October 5th. Thank you Mr. Longshore for your willingly professional and very friendly and helpful assistance in providing the author with vital data as to the most common native tree species found in the Muskogee County area.

The author would like to thank ALL THE MODELS found in the final artistic art format photographs produced by the author in this novel for presenting their God given bodily images willingly. ¡Gracias! ...y que Dios santísimo siga bendiciéndolos en donde se encuentren... ¡en ésta o la próxima vida!

Finally, thank you to these photographers for their free use original images used in the artwork by the author in this novel: Gerhard G; Sipa; Marcel Langthim; Thomas G; Cottonbro; Warren K Leffler; Polina Tankilevitch, Andrew; Ottoni Lu Ottoni; Andrea Piacquadio; Alvin C. Kraenzlein; H.Hach; Dan Evans; Andi Ravsanjani Gusma; Anete Lusi; Elijah O'Donnell; Luiz Fernando; Julia Volk; Rodnae Productions; Sam Lion; Hamed Almari; Quintin Gellar; Hassan Ouajbir; Ba Tik; Eunhyuk Ahn; David Mark; Armin Rimoldi; Artem Beliaikin; Victoria Boirodinova; Zorro Zombie; Heyn & Matzen image of Joseph Two Bulls; Erika Wittlieb; Ian Beckley; Miriam Espacio; Min An; João Cabral; Edward S. Curtis Piegan; John Vachon; Timothy H. O'Sullivan; Zinpix; Yan Krukov; Neto Soares; David De Giovanni;Alexander Krivitskiy; Bhargava Marripati; Raul Juarez; Ricardo Esquivel; Andreza Vasconcelos; Burak Fatih;Jonathan Borba; Katerina Holmes; Kathryn Archibald; Daria Shevtsova; Ketut Subiyanto; Matheus Bertelli; Meru Bi; Pavel Danilyuk; Anna Shvets; Tatiana Twinslol; Mateus Souza; and a thank you to the Brazilian National Archives; and Fenno Jacobs. ¡Gracias!

And thank you readers for taking the time to read something different!...and hopefully something that will help transform your lives to serve your community better, and to find contentment in small actions for a better world!

Sincerely,

Mi'Kha-el Feeza

This novel is also dedicated to

Salvador Guillermo Allende Gossens

A visionary in a contaminated world. A man who chose to push rather than be pushed. A man whose human-intent was to better conditions to his constituents *before-his-own.*

image in public domain courtesy of the National Archives of Brazil

oT eht stsinataS taht elur eht dlrow: potS gniyalp sa fi sretsefinam-fo-a-enod-laed. oN slaed evah neeb deifidilos; on sraw evah neeb now. oN egaugnal detaerc lliw reted na-dne-ot-ruoy-emag. cigaM dna sllepS era sloot fo a naicigam...a tcudorp fo eslaf sesimorp...a gniralf thgil gnimoc ot sti elzzif!

elzzif elzzif elzzif

tahW si fo nam? *tahW si fo* nuS? *tahW si fo* lasrevinU yrotirreT?: a mroftalp tuohtiw elbats dnuorg!

...A gnihsem fo seigrene ot eb ylenif desuffid dna denethgiarts rof gnissecorp kcab ot rieht *nigiro*....gnisol lla lortnoc fo noilleber.

noilleber: ylleb pu!

ehT seirotcaf era gnimoc ot a esolc...lla stnemele gnieb nekater rof *eht-gnisolc-fo-eht-rood!*

ecnO eht rooD si tuhS...

...ereht si oN-nruteR

osergeron

About The Author

No. The Author is not Full of Shit! [Well: maybe sometimes, temporarily, after eating:)]

The author is from Santa Monica, California. He is (among many things like most of us) a musician, visual artist, and literary writer. This may be his very first and very last trilogy writings in terms of "a novel" for many reasons that go beyond his control.

Mi'Kha-el Feeza is a graduate from the University of California, Los Angeles with a degree in history. He is also a graduate from Loyola Marymount University, Los Angeles with a master degree in education. Mi'Kha-el Feeza attended college under an assumed name!

J

Jana was written by the author from 2007 to 2018, with final editorial revisions from 2019 to November 2020 (13 years of writing to complete) in the following locations:

- Harvey Bay, Queensland, Australia
- Santa Monica, California
- Malibu, California
- San Diego, California
- San Francisco, California
- Oahu, Hawaii
- Kauai, Hawaii
- Pacific Ocean, 700 miles from Kona on a Hawaiian Airlines Aircraft
- Tulsa, Oklahoma
- Tucson, Arizona
- Grand Junction, Colorado
- Baltimore, Maryland
- "Agantao" The Tin Can [my exile]
- Strange Town
- Crenshaw/Coliseum Streets in LA
- The Lazy Living Room: Larchmont Village

...villagers [these and the like around the world] you are allowed to Awaken! Look around you, breathe, and see beyond your own comforts! Yes villagers: others exist that need your help! ¡Vámonos! True Help Not Crumbs. Need an Incentive: By Helping Others You Help Yourselves! J

- City of Bell (one hour afternoon)
- Seattle, Washington
- Whittier, California